Big Mama Stories

Big Mama Stories

by

Eleanor Arnason

Seattle

Aqueduct Press, PO Box 95787
Seattle, WA 98145-2787
www.aqueductpress.com

ISBN: 978-1-61976-029-5
Library of Congress Control Number: 2013932862
10 9 8 7 6 5 4 3 2 1

Cover painting: "Promise," courtesy Ta-coumba Aiken
Copyright © Ta-coumba Aiken

Book Design by Kathryn Wilham

Acknowledgments

"Big Ugly Mama and the ZK" was first published in *ASIMOV'S*,
September 2003.

"Big Black Mama and Tentacle Man" was first published in *Tales of
the Unanticipated* #24, July 2003.

"Big Green Mama Falls in Love" was first published in *Eidolon I*,
June 2006, eds. Jeremy G. Byrne and Jonathan Strahan, Eidolon
Publications

Printed in the USA by Thomson Shore, Inc.

For Timmi Duchamp, Kath Wilham, and
Tom Duchamp at Aqueduct Press,
with many thanks

Contents

BIG BLACK MAMA AND TENTACLE MAN

One day Big Black Mama was walking along, minding her own business, walking up and down over the rises and through the valleys that mass makes in space. She took care to stay away from really massive objects, big stars and large black holes, so the gravity slopes she climbed were comfortable, just right for a saunter.

The galaxy was all around her like a great swirl of diamond dust; and at her ankles—zip! zip!—were the STL ships of people who didn't know about FTL. She watched carefully, stepping over or around the ships. Not a single one hit her in the ankle, which was a good thing, since they could deal a nasty shock, if they were going fast enough. Not to mention what her ankle would do to them.

Big Black Mama kept walking along, enjoying the crisp, cold vacuum and faint popping noise that particles make as they go in and out of existence. Maybe she wasn't paying enough attention to where she was going. In any case, she came around a big, dark cloud of interstellar dust; and there was Tentacle Man, twice as tall as she was and ugly as oppression.

"My, you are a fine looking woman," he said.

This was true. Big Black Mama was tall as the sky and black as space. Her eyes shone like a pair of G2 suns. Her lips were as wide and red as the tulip fields on the planet of New Holland. The best melons in existence—giant, mutant, hybrid Persians—could not compare with her breasts for size and firmness. As for her hips and thighs, there were no adequate metaphors—though walls, towers, mountains, and planetoids came to mind. The best part of her was her brain.

Tentacle Man went on. "Just looking at you makes me want to ravish all your orifices with my tentacles and then eat you with my big mouth full of ichor-dripping fangs."

"Why would you want to do that?" Big Black Mama asked, gauging the situation. Tentacle Man looked fast and mean to her, but he didn't look smart.

"The universe is large, dark, cold, uncaring, and dangerous," said Tentacle Man. "There's no place in it for people who can't do the math and figure the odds."

"We're not talking about the universe," said Big Black Mama. "We're talking about you."

"Well, then," said Tentacle Man. "I want to do it, and I can do it. That's reason enough." He slithered forward on his tentacles, opening his mouth wide to show the ichor-dripping fangs. It was a nasty sight. The man could use a dentist.

His dental care was not Big Black Mama's problem; but his intentions were. She held up a hand authoritatively. "Wait just a minute! If you think I'm a morsel, you ought to see my sister, Big White Mama. Everyone agrees she's prettier than I am. For one thing, I'm fat. Big White Mama has curves; I'd be lying if I said otherwise. But she doesn't have bulges." Big Black Mama tapped her hip to demonstrate what a bulge was.

"You look fine to me," said Tentacle Man. "There's more to savor." And he slithered a little closer on his tentacles.

"Well, then," said Big Black Mama quickly. "You must have noticed that all truly refined and civilized people, the ones with the very best taste, are pale."

Tentacle Man, who had every nasty color you can imagine on his spotty, grotty skin, looked puzzled.

"It's true," said Big Black Mama firmly. "If you want elegance and delicacy and a really good flavor, go for the white meat! It's always best. Human men know this. Ain't one of them alive who doesn't start barking when Big White Mama lets down her golden hair."

Tentacle Man considered. "That may be, but she's not here, and you are."

"If you let me, I'll go get her and bring her here," said Big Black Mama.

"I may look stupid," said Tentacle Man. (He did.) "But I won't fall for that. As soon as I let you go, you'll run off so quickly that you'll shift from black to red; and I will never see you again."

"Let me send her a message," Big Black Mama said. "It won't take long. She's sure to come. In the meantime, we can play poker."

"What's poker?" asked Tentacle Man.

"It's a game of memory and mathematics. I'm sure a clever man like you will do just fine at playing it."

As Big Black Mama suspected, Tentacle Man was not bright; but he was greedy and vain. The thought of having two beautiful women to ravish and eat appealed a lot. He wasn't worried about them ganging up on him, because he had a high opinion of his strength and intelligence. The idea of learning poker appealed to him as well. He liked games, and he thought he was good at them, especially ones that involved math.

So Tentacle Man agreed, and Big Black Mama sent a message to her sister. She used tachyons. The message traveled faster than light into the past. It arrived at Big White Mama's house long, long before it was sent and set off her transtemporal alarm. This was a nifty gadget, which all the Big Sisters had, so they would know when anything interesting was happening and could go take a look. Big White Mama was home. Of course she took a look.

In the meantime, Big Black Mama pulled out a pack of cards and showed Tentacle Man how to play poker. It was hard work, because he was dumb as a brick. But Big Black Mama was an A-1 poker player and made sure he won most of the hands. This kept him busy for while. In the end, however, he got restless and began to look horny and hungry. Just then, when Big Black Mama was starting to worry, Big White Mama arrived. She had taken a shortcut through time and space, because the message sounded serious.

"Yo, girl," she said to Big Black Mama. "What kind of trouble you got yourself in this time?"

Tentacle Man's beady little eyes bugged out till it seemed he must have eye stalks. Big White Mama was something to view! Her eyes were blue and shone like a pair of Class O stars. Her cheekbones were razor-sharp ridges. Her mouth was fresh and lovely as a field of pale pink tulips opening in a northern spring. Her golden hair hung over her fine, tight ass. Her breasts were as round and smooth as the best giant mutant hybrid apples. As good as everything else was, her best part was her brain.

"This is Tentacle Man," said Big Black Mama. "He wants to eat you."

Tentacle Man began to slither forward on his tentacles, still holding his cards.

"You know," said Big White Mama. "This is not a good idea. Everyone says I'm pale, insipid, and over-civilized. I have no Soul. I have no fire and passion. The music I play is boring. I can hardly dance."

"I don't want to dance with you," said Tentacle Man irritably. "I want to eat you." He noticed he was still holding the cards and lifted his tentacle to toss them away.

"Don't do that," said Big Black Woman. "I think you've got a winning hand."

Tentacle Man paused, looking confused, and kept the cards (five jokers) in his tentacle.

"What you want," said Big White Mama, "is my sister Big Red Mama. Wild meat has the best flavor; and brother, she is wild!"

"Big White Mama has a point," said Big Black Mama. "Red's my sister, too. She is fiery and also respectful of men. That's a fault that White and I share. We just aren't respectful. But Red likes a warrior, a guy with machismo."

"What's machismo?" asked Tentacle Man.

"A big penis," said Big White Woman.

Tentacle Man looked worried.

"Or big tentacles" said Big Black Mama. "That will do just as well. We can see you have those all over."

Tentacle Man looked proud. Then he frowned. "But she isn't here, and you two are." He glanced from one to the other, trying to decide which woman looked more tasty.

Just then, as he was looking back and forth and having a hard time making up his tiny mind, Big Red Mama came walking around the dust cloud. Big White Mama had sent her a message, which had gone a hundred million years into the past. By a curious coincidence, that's where Red happened to be, wading through a lush Cretaceous marsh and looking at dinosaurs. They were her favorite animals. The message from Big White Mama said, "Trouble." So Red took a quick trip through time and space and arrived not even breathing heavily.

"Yo, sisters," she said. "What kind of trouble have got yourselves in now?"

Tentacle Man's beady eyes bugged out again. Beyond any question Big Red Mama was a vision—as tall as her sisters with fire-red skin and hair that fell to her ankles like black rain. Her eyes were dark and deep as space. Her lips were as red as Big Black Mama's. As for her breasts— well, there are no words for them, except maybe zkfzl, which isn't in any human language. (In the language of the Zk, it means a sight so remarkable that you will instantly meta-morphosize into your next life-stage upon seeing it.)

Not being Zk, Tentacle Man remained his ugly self. He was starting to become uneasy. The three big women stood on three sides of him, and he couldn't keep them all in view. Granted, they were female and all so lovely that his mating tentacle became painfully engorged. But put together they massed more than he did; and he was beginning to notice how tough they looked—their eyes flashing like stars or comets, their feet set wide, and their long, strong legs re-minding him of space elevators rising up and up and up.

"You know," said Big Red Mama in a soft, husky, friendly voice. "We come from a large family, and I sent for the rest of us as soon as I got my sister's message. Here they come."

Zap! Big Yellow Mama arrived. Zap! Big Brown Mama arrived. Then the rest came—as many colors as a rain-bow, since humans had evolved a lot as they spread out across the stars. There was a sky-blue Mama, a grass-green Mama, a Mama as deep red as burgundy wine, a Mama as orange as sunset, an indigo Mama like the deep blue, briny oceans of Earth. On and on the arriving went, till Tentacle Man was surrounded by a wall of Big Mamas. Now he was really nervous.

"I meant no harm," he said through closed lips, so no one could see his ichor-dripping fangs. "I was just kidding. I wouldn't ravish and eat anyone as lovely as you ladies."

Just then Big Ugly Mama arrived. She was larger than all the rest; and she wasn't pretty, though she was smart. She loomed over her sisters and glowered down at Tentacle Man. "WOULD YOU RAVISH AND EAT ME?' she boomed.

Tentacle Man cowered down, most of his tentacles over his spotty, grotty head. "I wouldn't think of it," he whimpered.

Big Ugly Mama reached down and picked him up by the scruff of his spotty, grotty neck. "I THINK YOU'RE LYING ABOUT YOUR INTENTIONS."

"No! No!" cried Tentacle Man. "I wouldn't harm you! Why, you're just like me! Neither one of us is a looker, though I think we both have character."

Big Ugly Mama laughed her booming laugh. "UGLY IS AS UGLY DOES. I MAY HAVE MY FAULTS, BUT I DON'T THINK WE HAVE A LOT IN COMMON." Then she knotted all his tentacles together — making him into a spotty, grotty, lumpy ball — and tossed him into the center of the interstellar dust cloud.

They could hear him shouting and thrashing around inside, but they had no pity, because the universe *is* large, dark, cold, uncaring, and dangerous; and our only hope and help is one another. If you don't recognize the bond that ties intelligent life together, and if you try to use the universe as an excuse for your antisocial behavior — well, you deserve what you get.

All the Mamas grinned and gave each other high fives; and then they went off to the end of time to party, which they did well, as they do everything they do.

> Note: In case you are wondering, there are Big Poppas. They are as large and smart and colorful as the Mamas; and all these wonderful, colorful people love each other dearly. But the Big Poppas don't come into this story.

BIG UGLY MAMA AND THE ZK

One day Big Ugly Mama was walking along, minding her own business, admiring how the galaxy looked spread out around her, the stars shining red, yellow, white, and blue.

"Nothing is finer than a well-made, well-run galaxy," she said to no one in particular. "Though that black hole in the middle bothers me sometimes."

But she didn't want to think about the black hole eating away, eating away at all the shoals and fields of lovely stars; so she didn't. She was a woman of character and could regulate her mind.

As she was going along, she noticed a star ship in her way. She could tell by the design that it was FTL, but it wasn't doing any FTLing at the moment. Instead it was floating, dark and unpowered, right where she was likely to stub her toe on it.

She bent down and picked it up, turning it in her hands. Zk work. She could tell because it had windows. The Zk liked windows and put them in all their ships, though there wasn't much to see in FTL travel.

She lifted the ship to one of her big, ugly eyes and peered inside. It was a one-person racer, and she was looking into the single cabin. The emergency power system was on. A few lights shone dimly. The cabin's single seat was occupied by the best-looking male Zk she had ever seen. He was in the fifth life-stage, full and glorious maturity. His carapace shone like bronze; his belly was a delicate shade of yellow; his feathery antennae were azure; and his eight segmented limbs were as brightly red as freshly spilled human blood.

"YO," Big Ugly mama said in her booming voice. "ARE YOU ALL RIGHT IN THERE?"

The Zk opened his four emerald-green eyes. "No," he warbled. "My FTL engines have failed, and I'm stranded in normal space. This is an especially serious problem, because I'm due home to be crowned king of all the Zk."

"HMM," said Big Ugly Mama.

The Zk prince climbed out of the pilot's seat and made his way to a window. He wanted to know who was outside. You don't meet a lot of people in a vacuum. All he could see was an eye with a mud-brown iris and a blood-shot white. "Could you step back, so I can see you?" he asked politely.

Big Ugly Mama thought for a moment, then extended her big, strong, ugly arm so the ship was at arm's length. The Zk prince looked out and saw her.

There are two things you need to know in order to understand what followed.

First, the Zk are a highly visual species, as might be expected from their four eyes; and the metamorphoses that move them from one life-stage to another are, at least in part, visually triggered. Zk scientists believe this reliance on visual cues developed so the Zk could synchronize their life-stages with their planet's Long Year. Most likely, the scientists say, the original triggers were sunlight, length of day, changing weather, and the colors of the Zk Long Seasons.

Over millennia of civilization the Zk have learned to respond to a wide range of visual stimuli; and the strength of their visual experiences can either speed up or slow down their progress through life. As a result, the Zk are careful about what they look at. Their cities, gardens, and countrysides provide an unending series of calm, pleasant vistas; their art is soothing; and they always prefer the beautiful to the sublime — unless they are planning to go to war. Then they expose their third-stage adolescents to bad weather, savage wildernesses, and disturbing art. This shocks the surly kids into molting; and they emerge as fourth-stage warriors.

Got that?

The second thing you need to know is how ugly Big Ugly Mama was. This is not easy to describe. "Plain as a rock" and "ugly as a mud fence" do not begin to convey the right idea. Her ugliness was primeval — like cooling lava on a planet not yet entirely formed, or like broad, empty mud flats on a world where no life has yet emerged from the ocean. It was a fundamental homeliness, full of potential. Imagine her as a mountain of manure — enough to fertilize a hundred thousand gardens and make them flourish, but as yet unused. Along with all this, she looked like a human woman.

Does this help you form an image?

The Zk prince got an eyeful, and it was a nasty experience. He shrieked with horror, dropped to the cabin floor, and curled into a ball. The meta-pores that covered his carapace extruded a shiny white goo. This spread over his entire surface, rapidly hardening. Within minutes, he was encased in a kind of egg.

"OH DEAR," said Big Ugly Mama in her booming voice. This was her fault. She should have remembered how sensitive the Zk were. In her defense, it has to be said that the galaxy is full of intelligent species, all with their individual quirks. It's hard for anyone to remember every little idiosyncrasy.

In any case, she couldn't leave the Zk in an unpowered ship in the middle of nowhere, especially in his current vulnerable condition. So she tucked the ship in a pocket and headed for the Zk home planet. This was going to be mighty hard to explain. The Zk were expecting a handsome fifth-stage prince, not a premature sixth-stage brooder; and they weren't going to be happy. It's hard to crown a person who's covered with spines and wants to be underwater, caring for the next generation.

She walked along and walked along, paying careful attention to where she put her feet. There were a lot of species that didn't know about FTL. Their STL ships whizzed around her ankles. They'd give her a nasty jab if they hit. But none did. After a while, she heard a cracking sound in her shirt pocket. The Zk was hatching. She took the ship out and peered inside.

The pseudo-egg lay in pieces on the cabin floor. But instead of a spiny brooder she expected to see, there was a sullen, unattractive grub.

"HOLY TOLEDO," said Big Ugly Mama or something to the same effect. The sight of her had driven the Zk prince into metamorphasizing *backwards*; and he was now a third stage adolescent.

You may say this is impossible. The arrow of time goes in one direction only. This shows you don't know much about the galaxy's Mamas, who live by their own rules.

"YO?" said Big Ugly Mama in a tone of timid inquiry.

"Fuck you," said the grub.

It was still male. She could tell because it had a semen depositor, which was erect. Erotic dreams in the egg, she supposed.

"MIND YOUR TONGUE, YOUNG MAN," she boomed.

The semen depositor shrank out of sight. The grub cringed and said, "Yes, m'am."

"DO YOU REMEMBER WHO YOU ARE?"

The grub frowned, thinking. "Glory of the Zk Five," he said and glanced at his reflection in a window.[1] "But I'm not a five!"

"YOU GOT THAT RIGHT," boomed Big Ugly Mama. She found it interesting that he'd kept his memory. Well, the Zk kept their memories when they metamorphasized forward. All this told her was the present dilemma was caused by biology, not time travel. Thinking this gave her a wisp of an idea.

"What happened?" cried the grub.

"FIRST OF ALL, PULL YOUR BLINDS." Her booming voice brooked no opposition, even from an adolescent. The grub pulled the blinds, and Big Ugly Mama explained the situation.

"This is your fault!" cried the grub. "You have ruined my life! I'm going to sue."

"YOU CAN'T SUE A BIG MAMA, ANY MORE THAN YOU CAN SUE A FORCE OF NATURE."

"That's unfair!"

....

1 By now you are probably wondering why the Zk put windows in their space ships, if they are so sensitive to what they see. Very little in interstellar space disturbs them. An exploding star is merely splendid if it has no planets with life. Horror and terror require a human (or Zk) context. In addition, all Zk windows have blinds.

"WOULD YOU PLEASE BE QUIET, SO I CAN THINK? I HAVE THE WISP OF AN IDEA."

There was silence behind the drawn blinds, except for some scuffling and muffled slams. The grub being petulant, Big Ugly Mama supposed. She stood with the ship in one hand, looking at a very nice ring nebula. A dim spark glowed in the center, the remains of what must have been one heck of a star. Her big, ugly brow wrinkled. She thought.

For the most part, Big Ugly Mama avoided time travel. Why go back? You already know what's happened. Why forward? It ruins the surprise. But like all Big Mamas, she could travel in time.

She couldn't think of another way to solve the current problem. It was too risky to try scaring the Zk forward to stage five. If the same thing happened again, she'd have a very large big baby (conservation of matter) or something worse.

This was her fault. She owed the Zk their stage-five prince. She was going to have to take the grub back in time and raise him to full maturity; and she couldn't involve any Zk in the process. For one thing, she didn't want to go through the embarrassment of explaining what she'd done. For another, the prince already existed in the past; and involving Zk—who might know him and certainly would know about him—could lead to a paradox. Since she had never taken an interest in time travel, she wasn't really sure what caused paradoxes, but she did not want one. They were messy and hard to clean up.

At least the grub could think after a fashion. She could explain her plan to him and ask for his help.

She did. He groaned and moaned and said, "Fuck it!"

She couldn't blame him for this reaction. Adolescence was awful in every species. No rational being would want to go through it twice. Young adulthood could be bad, too, though many enjoyed it.

"IT HAS TO BE," said Big Ugly Mama firmly.

Mumble. Moan. Sigh. "Okay."

She carried him into the past, ship and all. As she was traveling, it occurred to her that she might as well go some-when interesting, since she was going to be stuck then for twenty human years or so. She liked dinosaurs a lot; all the Big Mamas did; but they'd almost certainly scare the grub. She decided on Earth in the early Carboniferous. Plants had emerged from the ocean and covered the land. That would make the era seem more attractive to a Zk than earlier eras. While animals had followed — or possibly preceded — the plants to land, most of them were comparatively small and unalarming. She thought she remembered that the Carboniferous had cockroaches and dragonflies. These shouldn't brother the grub. He had looked a bit like a cockroach in stage five.

The scary creatures were in rivers and the oceans; and the Zk were not aquatic, except in their first and sixth stages. They didn't even swim or wade in shallow water, when in a body without gills. Her charge ought to be safe.

She arrived in a forest in the middle of a hot afternoon. The trees tickled her ankles. She downsized a bit, so she fit in the landscape better. A dragonfly flitted past. Its body was iridescent green, and its half-meter long wings were transparent.

"VERY NICE," said Big Ugly Mama to herself. She could no longer carry the Zk ship in one hand. Instead, she put it over a shoulder and trudged along, her big ugly feet sinking deep into the marshy ground. The air was full of unfamiliar aromas; the trees she walked among were distinctly odd. One kind had no branches. Instead, its segmented trunk rose straight up, tapering as it rose. Green tufts grew between the segments.[2]

Another variety had a trunk that split into a single pair of branches. Each branch ended in a bunch of long, narrow, grass-like leaves, which hung down limply, moving slightly in a humid breeze.[3] To Big Ugly Mama, both kinds looked tentative, as if the plants in question hadn't yet figured out a good way to be big. There weren't enough branches or enough leaves, and the leaves weren't broad enough or angled properly. How much sunlight does a leaf get, when it hangs straight down? Neither kind would last a year, competing with more modern trees.

A third variety seemed to be doing a better job, having complicated, fern-like leaves; but they grew directly out of the trunk, forming a cluster at the top of the tree. The trunk was covered with diamond-shaped scales. Big Ugly Mama was pretty certain these were scars left when leaves dropped off. The tree must begin its life looking like a true fern. Then, as it grew, the trunk pushed the cluster of leaves higher and higher toward sunlight, till the entire plant was twenty or thirty meters tall.[4] It was a pretty good solution for how to get light in a forest.

Only the undergrowth plants were familiar to her: true ferns and scouring rushes. These plants had figured out the right way to be their size and had survived into later ages.

....

2 *Calamites*, related to modern-day horse tails or scouring rushes.

3 *Sigillaria*, related to modern-day club mosses.

4 *Lepidodendron*, another club moss relative.

She squelched along, the ship on her shoulder, trying to put a mental finger on the place's true strangeness. Finally, she got it. The forest was silent. No birds sang, of course; and there weren't the bug and animal noises that a Permian or Jurassic forest would produce. Even the leaves rustled quietly, as if afraid of awaking the future.

"Are we there?" asked the grub behind his blinds.

"YES, THOUGH I'M NOT SURE YOU OUGHT TO RISK LOOKING OUT YET." She glanced at the ground, where something was moving. "HOW DO YOU FEEL ABOUT TWO METER LONG, MULTI-SEGMENTED ANIMALS WITH MANY LEGS?"

"What color are they?"

"THIS ONE IS BURNT SENNIA."

"Sounds fine to me. The Zk keep animals like that as pets."

This *was* the right place, Big Ugly Mama thought. She climbed a long slope out of the forest and stopped on a hilltop. The ground was dry; the plants were low; and she had an excellent view of the forest, stretching east through hazy sunlight. Water gleamed at the horizon: a large lake or the ocean.

"J'Y SUIS, J'Y RESTE,"[5] said Big Ugly Mama and put the Zk star ship down.

"Can I come out now?" asked the grub.

....

5 This is French and means, "I'm here, I'm staying here." Like all Mamas, Big Ugly Mama was self-educated. She had learned a lot in the course of a long life and was especially good at quotes and tag lines, though she didn't always understand exactly what they meant. In this case she did know.

"JUST A MOMENT," said Big Ugly Mama. She downsized further and hid in a small, unfamiliar plant. "OKAY."

The grub opened the door and stood a moment in sunlight, blinking his four emerald-green eyes. A small myriapod, about ten centimeters long, noticed Big Ugly Mama and decided to eat her. She socked it in the head. Due to conservation of matter, it was one heck of a punch. The bug fell dead. She felt bad about killing it and a little worried about paradoxes; but the death of a bug in the Carboniferous was not likely to change the future. Time is a lot fuzzier than people think and tends to be self-correcting over long periods.

Think of each moment as a particle vibrating within a specific range, which overlaps with the ranges of the before and after moments. Every instant we experience consists of *now*, a bit of *now + 1* and a bit of now of *now - 1*. It's this overlap that makes time continuous and enables the individual moments to transmit information from one to another. The information tends to go forward, but there is a slight contrary movement, which is why people sometimes react to things before they happen.

The grub stepped out of the ship and took a deep breath. "It tastes good." He glanced around. "It looks good. But twenty years is a long time."

"DID YOU BRING ANY BOOKS?"

"My ship library has a complete collection of Zk classics, none of which I've read."

"THERE YOU ARE. YOU CAN SPEND THE NEXT TWENTY YEARS GETTING AN EDUCATION."

The grub groaned.

This is a short story, so I'm not going to describe the next ten years in detail. Big Ugly Mama built a cabin for herself next to the star ship. When the grub was out and about, she stayed inside or hid in a plant. The myriapods continued to bother her, but this problem declined over time. Did they have a way to communicate? Could they learn from the mistakes of others? She didn't know.

The grub spent his days hiking and studying the biology of Earth. A lovely planet, he told Big Ugly Mama, full of wonderful bugs. Often he brought specimens home. Cockroaches were especially numerous and varied, ranging in size from teeny tiny to half a meter long. They came in many attractive colors and had many interesting habits. He learned the Zk system of scientific naming and named them all.

At night he pulled his blinds and read Zk classics or talked with Big Ugly Mama. She expanded to her full size—which was a wonderful relief; being small gave her cramps—and sat out under the Carboniferous stars, breathing the soft, warm, night air. Above her meteors blazed into Earth's atmosphere, many of them brilliant. She didn't worry. This wasn't a period that had mass extinctions.

At the end of ten years, the grub molted into a shiny, gray warrior. For the most part, this was a good change. His moods improved, and he argued less. He became more independent, spending days away in the forest or along the nearby ocean shore. Now he discovered what lived in the water, finding their remains on the ocean beaches and bringing these home: wonderful, shimmery nautaloid shells; shark teeth; trilobite carapaces; and plates from armored fish. Big Ugly Mama told him what she knew about evolution on Earth. He was glad to miss the dinosaurs, though—being a warrior—he was less timid than he'd been as a grub or a prince.

Big Ugly Mama took trips as well. Hers were in both time and space. It wasn't easy, being stuck in the Age of Plants and Coal with a Zk kid.

One day, coming back from a visit to the Cretaceous, she saw something standing by her cabin. It was twice as tall as the cabin and covered with sharp, nasty-looking spines. The moment she laid eyes on it, she knew it didn't belong here and now. She upsized till she was as big as the thing and asked, "WHAT ON EARTH ARE YOU?"

"I'm a Stage Six Zk Big Mama," the thing replied. "And not usually found on Earth. The Zk crown prince is missing. I tracked him here. A nice place! I've spent some time exploring and watching you. It's always a good idea to look around before acting. Now." She upsized till she was twice as tall as Big Ugly Mama. "What is going on, you nasty-looking thing? Why have you stolen our prince? Why did you bring him here? And why has he gone back to being a warrior?"

Big Ugly Mama upsized as well. They stared at one another, green eyes glaring at mud brown.

Big Ugly Mama had a lot of self-confidence, but she didn't like the look of those spines. So she was the first one to blink. She took a step back to see what would happen. The Zk Big Mama stayed put, which meant she was looking for information rather than a fight.

Big Ugly Mama explained what had happened.

"My," said the Zk Big Mama when she finished. "What a story! As I said, I've been watching him and you. He seems to be doing well, in spite of being one stage behind himself. Apparently you have done a good job of raising him through grubhood."

Big Ugly Mama said, "I HAVE GROWN TO LOVE HIM, THOUGH HE WAS VERY TRYING AS A GRUB."

"They all are."

They downsized and sat in front of the cabin, getting to know one another. Night fell. So did a splendid meteor shower. It was sublime, but the Zk Big Mama was too tough to molt or form an egg.

They watched the shower in silence till the last red fireball vanished and then were silent for a while longer, considering what they had seen. Finally the Zk Big Mama spoke. "The obvious solution is for me to go forward in time and grab the prince shortly before he meets you. But then we'd lose the person he has become due to you. As handsome as he was—or will be—in stage five, he was not an ideal crown prince. Surely you noticed this! He ran off alone in a one-person racer when he was due to be crowned, and he never studied anything except FTL racing. As he was the moment you met him, he boded fair to be an ignorant, self-indulgent monarch. No treat for the Zk!"

The Zk Big Mama paused, and Big Ugly Mama felt good about helping the Zk prince. Maybe it hadn't been a mistake to let him see her. She had brooded over this, though—having a well regulated mind—she hadn't brooded often or for long.

"I could take him as he is now and carry him forward to the coronation. But he'd be too young to be crowned. No species in its right mind gives power to warriors."

Was that true? Big Ugly Mama wondered.

"I could take him to a point in time ten years or so before the coronation. Then he could grow naturally into a stage-five prince. But there are several problems with this. For one thing there would be two identical princes in the same time-frame. Which prince would be the true heir? What if they met? Being stage four, both would be feisty. Neither would back down. We'd have a fight and maybe a war."

Would a war over the Zk succession be a paradox? Big Ugly Mama wondered. Or merely a royal mess?

"I could try shocking him into stage five — I admit I'm a little worried, due to your experience; but I think that was more you than him. You are really quite amazingly ugly! I'm almost certain I could find something that would frighten him forward into the next stage of his life. Myself, maybe." She smiled, revealing many long, pointed teeth.

This sounded like the best idea so far. Big Ugly Mama said as much.

"It has flaws," the Zk Big Mama said. "He will miss ten years of his life."

"HE SPENT TEN YEARS AS A WARRIOR BEFORE HE MET ME."

"Yes; but in a sense that prince no longer exists, except in the future. We are the products of experience, and the boy we have here has been through many experiences that the former/future prince did not—or has not—or will not have."

Big Ugly Mama remembered why she disliked time travel. It was hell on tenses.

"Why reinvent the wheel or meddle with success?" the Zk Mama asked suddenly.

What? thought Big Ugly Mama.

"You raised him through grubhood and were ready to bring him through stage four. His experiences have made him a fine warrior. With your help, he stands a good chance of becoming a fine prince." The Zk Big Mama turned stiffly. Apparently her neck and shoulder spines interfered with flexibility. Four green eyes regarded Big Ugly Mama beseechingly. "Would you be willing to stay here with him till he molts?"

Big Ugly Mama looked out across the Carboniferous forest. The sun was a line of fire at the horizon, and the forest was turning from black to green. A few wisps of mist hung above the tree tops. They had talked the whole way through the night. Did she want to stay here and mentor the warrior? She wasn't certain. She needed time to think. "IT'S HIS LIFE. SHOULDN'T WE CONSULT WITH HIM BEFORE MAKING A DECISION?"

The Zk Big Mama considered while scratching a particularly nasty-looking spine. "I suppose it wouldn't hurt to ask. A warrior can think fairly well, except about war. You said it might be several days before he comes back here. I'm going to pay a visit to the ocean. I've been out of water too long. My spines are getting itchy."

"THERE ARE NASTY THINGS IN THE WATER HERE."

"I know that already. I stopped in a river when I arrived. A five-meter-long, carnivorous amphibian tried to eat me. I ate him. Time travel always makes me hungry. Don't worry about me."

It was one thing to kill an myriapod. They weren't in the human line of descent. But an amphibian could be the ancestor of humanity. She pointed this out to the Zk Big Mama.

"Hardly likely. It was too big and specialized. I'll be careful not to step on small tetrapods, if you are worried."

The Zk Big Mama left. Big Ugly Mama sat by herself, looking out over the forest. She had grown to love this era almost as much as she loved the boy. Let her count the ways! She loved the odd-looking trees; the dragonflies; the cockroaches; the life below the ocean surface, which she visited from time to time by diving. Nautiloids, trilobites, sharks, fields of crinoids like fields of lilies, reefs built by animals that were not corals.

Most of all, she loved the lack of animal sounds. When the wind was right, she could hear large amphibians roaring on the banks of rivers; and the little tetrapods peeped or trilled in their courting seasons; but most of the noise here came from wind, water, and foliage.

As Mamas went, she was relaxed. Why hurry through life, she thought, especially when Big Mamas had long, long lives. Ten years wouldn't make a lot of difference. A pair of courting dragonflies flew past her, their fire-red bodies coupled.

There was sex, of course. It had been a long time since she'd been with a Big Poppa. But that could wait. One thing about Big Poppas, if you wanted sex, they were always available and willing. She'd find one when she was ready.

Several days later, the warrior returned. He was carrying a small, dead shark; and it stank. "I forgot to take a stasis box," he said. "And my journey back took longer than I expected. It's gone a bit off."

"IT'S GONE A LOT OFF," said Big Ugly Mama, who was hiding in a plant.

"It happened so gradually that it didn't bother me much," said the warrior. "One must make sacrifices for science."

"PUT IT IN A STASIS BOX AND COME BACK OUT. I NEED TO TALK WITH YOU."

The warrior did so and sat down next to the plant. His gray shell gleamed in the late afternoon light. His eyes were still emerald-green. He had impressive pinchers and mandibles.

Big Ugly Mama explained the situation.

"My," said the warrior when she finished. "What a story! I always thought the Zk Big Mamas and Poppas were mythological. I should have known better after meeting you, I suppose. But none of the stories described any of the Mamas as looking like a huge human being who's been roughly shaped from excrement."

Big Ugly Mama did not get angry. The description was true; and ugly is as ugly does. Her big, strong heart was beautiful; and most of the time she remembered this; though even Big Mamas have occasional brief moments of doubt. "I'M A VERY SPECIAL HUMAN BIG MAMA," she told the warrior. "MORE *IN POSSE* THAN *IN ESSE*. MY COLLEAGUES, THE OTHER HUMAN BIG MAMAS, ARE MORE *IN ESSE* THAN *IN POSSE*."

"Say what?" asked the warrior.

"THE TERMS ARE FROM LATIN, AN ANCIENT HUMAN LANGUAGE; AND THE IDEAS ARE FROM ARISTOTLE, AN ANCIENT HUMAN THINKER."

"What do the terms mean?" asked the warrior asked.

"THEY'RE NOT IN YOUR TIME LINE, AND I'M NOT SURE YOU OUGHT TO KNOW—ESPECIALLY HERE AND NOW. WHO KNOWS WHAT HARM MIGHT OCCUR, THROUGH THE INTRODUCTION OF ARISTOTLE INTO THE CARBONIFEROUS?" There was another reason, which Big Ugly Mama didn't mention. She wasn't entirely 100% certain of the meaning of the terms.

The warrior persisted in asking. Finally Big Ugly Mama gave it her best try. "*ESSE* IS BEING. *POSSE* MEANS POSSIBILITY. THE OTHER MOTHERS ARE ABSOLUTELY, COMPLETELY AND PERFECTLY WHAT THEY ARE. I, ON THE OTHER HAND, AM A POTENTIAL MAMA OR A MAMA OF POTENTIAL. IMAGINE ME TO BE A SEED JUST SPROUTING OR A TADPOLE WITH TWO LEGS. OF COURSE I LOOK A LITTLE PECULIAR! NO MATTER WHEN I GO IN TIME, MY COMPLETE AND PERFECT SELF IS ALWAYS IN A FUTURE I NEVER REACH. I DON'T MIND THIS. TO ME, A JOURNEY IS ALWAYS MORE INTERESTING THAN THE DESTINATION IT AIMS AT; AND A REVOLUTION IS ALWAYS MORE INTERESTING—AND IMPORTANT—AND USEFUL—THAN THE SOCIETY IT DREAMS OF ESTABLISHING."

The warrior looked puzzled, which was hardly surprising, since the Zk did not have revolutions. He returned to the previous topic. "I can go home now and be crowned king of all the Zk?" he said.

"YES."

"I'll be a handsome prince again?"

"YES."

The warrior considered, frowning. "I'll lose ten years of my life."

"YOU LIVED THEM BEFORE," said Big Ugly Mama.

"But not here. I hated being a grub, but I like being a warrior. I'm brave and resourceful. I won't be, once I become a prince again. This is the toughest stage of life—

except for six, but all I'll care for then is the eggs I guard and the predators that menace them. This is the stage for exploration and self-expression, the stage for science and art and war." The warrior extended an arm and waved a pincher at the hazy forest. "I have an entire planet to explore and describe, not to mention the literature I may write. I've been scribbling poems lately, and I think I may be developing an individual voice."

"I GOT YOU INTO THIS SITUATION," said Big Ugly Mama. "IF YOU WANT TO STAY HERE, I'LL STAY AND KEEP YOU COMPANY."

The warrior was silent for a long time. Finally he said, "What I'd really like is a cadre of warriors, Zk compañeros who share my curiosity and courage."

What was the pang she felt? Relief that he didn't want her to stay with him? Or grief?

"I'LL SEE WHAT I CAN DO," said Big Ugly Mama.

The warrior went into his space ship. She stepped out of the plant and upsized till she was taller than a mountain. Clouds floated around her at shoulder-height, but they were widely scattered. She had no trouble seeing all the way to the ocean. The Zk Big Mama was there, sitting on the shore and eating a nautiloid with a two meter-long, conical shell. The shell lay next to her, and most of the nautiloid was in her mouth.

Big Ugly Mama dropped down to a reasonable size and took off through the forest of odd-looking trees. Soon she reached the ocean. A strong wind blew. Wild Carboniferous waves rolled in, crashing against one another, and surged up a beach of coarse, black sand. She walked along the beach, keeping an eye open for attractive shells and the carapaces of trilobites. There was something especially appealing about trilobites, though she wasn't certain what. The compact and elegant design of their bodies? Or their large compound eyes? They were the first creatures to take a really good look at life on Earth. That was worth prizing and praising.

At length she reached the Zk Big Mama. The nautiloid was gone except for its shell. The Zk Big Mama was examining this. "Very nice. What did the boy say?"

Big Ugly Mama told her.

"Typical of stage four. They are romantic, artistic, and violent. Four is the stage for art and war."

"IS IT POSSIBLE FOR HIM TO STAY HERE?"

"Yes."

"ALONE?"

"With Zk warrior companions."

'WON'T THAT CREATE A PARADOX?"

"It might, if this were the past of our home planet." The Zk Big Mama frowned, which she could do, because the spines on her forehead were small and flexible. "There might be paradoxes if the warriors I bring here gossip after they get home. The knowledge of time travel could change the Zk present."

The Zk Big Mama extruded a long, narrow, spiny-tipped tongue and licked out the nautiloid shell. Finally, after having gotten every morsel of flesh she could, she spoke again. "Either I will have to pick Zk warriors with very tight mandibles — or I will have to make sure the warriors in question do not return to the future."

"YOU CAN'T LEAVE THEM HERE!" Big Ugly Mama said, thinking of the repercussions of a Zk colony in Earth's past. It might not affect Zk history, but what if human paleontologists found fossils of bug-like space aliens in Carboniferous strata? It would delight the enemies of Darwin, and Big Ugly Mama liked Darwin. A nice, quiet, thoughtful man.

"I won't," said the Zk Big Mama. "Don't worry. This is my problem now. I'll take care of it." She rose and walked into the ocean, moving steadily out until the waves rolled around her, then over her. Then she was gone from sight.

Big Ugly Mama felt faintly dissatisfied. But the Zk Big Mama was right. This was a Zk problem, not a human one, and she was a human Big Mama. She went home to her cabin.

Some time later, the Zk Big Mama returned, bringing a troop ship full of hardy stage-four Zk. Big Ugly Mama bid farewell to the proto-prince and went forward to the future, which was her present or past. Damn time travel! She could never get her tenses right when doing it. For a while, she kept herself busy, doing one thing or another. But the proto-prince stayed on her mind. She missed him. She even missed him as a grub.

Finally, she went back to Earth in Carboniferous. The prince's racing ship was gone, and there was a note in her cabin, written in the most common human language. The letters were awkward, as if made by someone with stiff, spiny hands.

Your child has moved on. Don't try to find him. At a certain point in time (the early Carboniferous in this case) a boy has to break free of his mother. This is why first-stage Zk have razor-sharp baby mandibles. When the time is right, they can gnaw themselves free.

Thanks to you (and me) the coronation will take place when planned. Go then and see it and greet the Zk king, who is (in a sense) your son.

XXX,

The Zk Big Mama

P.S. In case you are wondering, I have moved the boy and his companions to the past of a planet that does not enter into Zk or human history. There are plenty of small animals with exoskeletons and odd-looking trees, so he shouldn't feel homesick for Earth. He can practice his taxonomy on an entirely new ecological system. The planet's night sky is amazing in a way I won't describe, since it might enable you to find the planet. With luck, it will inspire the boy to write good—or least adequate—poetry. It does a king no harm to write poems and study taxonomy. If done properly, both teach discipline and respect for the universe.

Unlike Earth in the Carboniferous, this planet does have some—though not many—large and dangerous land animals. The boy can test his mettle against these. A king should know something about courage, and it's better to learn courage by hunting than by war. Also, the hunting will help with his taxonomy. He and his warrior companions can hack a settlement out of the wilderness, which will keep them busy—busy pinchers are happy pinchers!—and teach him how to work with other people.

Poetry, taxonomy, courage, and cooperation! What better lessons can there be for a future king?

By the time he's ready to return to his native time and place, I will have decided what to do about his companions. If I mistrust the tightness of their mandibles, I'll leave them on the planet. There are both males and females in the group. They can form a colony and raise their children in the planet's warm, shallow, almost salt-free oceans. I suspect

the colony will evolve through genetic drift and an
environment that is different—and less hostile—than
the environment of the Zk home planet. Imagine
the variation that may develop, without the pruning
harshness of the Zk oceans and land! By the time
the prince is crowned, they will have become
something or many things unrecognizable as Zk.

Whatever happens, the human and Zk time lines
won't be disturbed.

XXX again.

Big Ugly Mama read the letter over a second time, then folded it with her big, strong, ugly hands. All's well that ends well, she thought. It was another of her quotes. She was still a little worried about the boy's companions. Leaving them on an alien planet seemed harsh to her. Couldn't the Zk Big Mama find a better solution?

Maybe not, and stage-six Zks were harsh. They had to be, in order to protect their children in the dangerous oceans of the Zk home planet.

Would the warriors evolve into a species without stage-six mothers and fathers? On a kinder world, stage six might not be necessary. If so, would new kinds of Big Mamas and Poppas appear, ones without spines and fangs and claws? An interesting idea! She would think about it later, since she had a suspicion it would give her a headache.

Better to think about missing the boy. That was an emotional problem, rather than a problem with the nature of existence; and unlike most existential problems, it could be solved. She would do what the Zk Big Mama suggested and go forward in time to the coronation. The boy she met then would not be the boy she missed now, but the two were closely related.

That would have to suffice. None of us, not even a Big Mama, can keep someone fixed at the specific stage or moment. The particles that make up time won't allow it. They want to vibrate and transmit information. Heraclitus noticed this a long time ago—or a long time in the future. A difficult man! Big Ugly Mama hadn't liked him. But he knew about stepping in rivers in ancient Greece. Here in the Carboniferous, he would most likely be eaten before he finished stepping in the same river once. Who knew what that would do to the history of human thought?

A slight pain appeared behind her eyes. She put the letter in a pocket and downsized herself. The day was bright and mild. Dragonflies flitted and shone around her. A two-meter-long myriapod was crawling slowly past her feet. Its back was as blue and speckled as a robin's egg. A good day to take a walk in the Carboniferous forest and then along a beach, while the wild Carboniferous waves rolled in. With luck, she'd find some good trilobite carapaces.

BIG GREEN MAMA FALLS IN LOVE

One day Big Green Mama was walking along, admiring the galaxy spread out around her, all the bright stars and nebulae. Her big green feet kicked up clouds of interstellar dust. Her big green lungs drew in vacuum and found it bracing. A good day for a long hike, she told herself. Maybe she would go all the way to Andromeda.

On and on she went, traveling through the valleys that mass makes in space and over the hills that rise between the valleys. At length, she came to one particular valley. It wasn't especially big or deep, but it had a pleasant look. A G2 star rested in the valley's center. Planets whizzed around the star. One of the planets shone blue and white. Big Green Mama knew what this meant; and she had always liked life. It was so active and full of surprises! She walked down the valley's slope till she reached the planet, then stopped, bent over, and took a peek. No question the planet was alive. The atmosphere smelled of oxygen. Green land showed between swirling weather systems. Some of the life was intelligent. She could tell this from the artificial satellites that whizzed around the planet. Big Green Mama smiled with pleasure. But then, after a moment or two of appreciating the racing satellites and green continents and—best of all—the tang of a living atmosphere, she noticed something was wrong.

All intelligent life is noisy. Any species able to travel in space is certain to produce lots of radiation of every kind. The planet should have been surrounded by signals. Instead, she heard and saw and felt silence.

There was a little chatter from the satellites, but they were machines, sending their reports automatically. Where were the people? Why were they quiet? Should she go down and find out what had happened? As she considered these questions, she began to look at the satellites, picking them up one by one and examining them closely, then putting them back in their orbits. No point in making a mess.

At length, she picked up a space telescope: a fine big one with a large mirror. As she examined it, she caught a glimpse of herself, lit by the G2 star and distorted by the mirror's curve. There isn't much that's big enough to reflect a Big Mama, and the telescope couldn't quite do the job. But she saw an eye with a dark green iris and a high, handsome cheek as green as young grass. Now, that was something! She took another look, admiring the eye and cheek. But it wasn't enough, and the distortion bothered her. So she took the mirror in her big green hands and flattened it out, then looked again. Much better, though she still couldn't see all of herself. She took hold of the mirror a second time and stretched it, till it was a shiny film. When she let it go, it floated in front of her like a silver curtain or sail. In time, the wind from the G2 star would blow it right out of this system. Meanwhile, she could see herself. What a fine, handsome woman she was! Eyes like emeralds, skin like grass, hair the deep shade of late-summer leaves. Her lips were like a pinkish-green orchid. She had a pair of full breasts, each as round as a planet, wide hips and legs that went on and on, till they ended in big, strong, good-looking green feet. Even her toes were handsome, since she never cramped them in shoes.

Staring at her reflection, Big Green Mama fell in love. This wasn't the kind of languid, romantic longing that got Narcissus in trouble, but a robust horniness. Looking at herself, Big Green Mama wanted to have sex.

Auto-eroticism was an option, but not one that interested her. She wanted to walk hand-to-hand with the person in the mirror, lie together on warm beaches, French kiss like crazy, marry, and settle down.

What was she going to do? She could go looking for a Big Poppa or another Big Mama, but she wasn't interested in just anyone. She wanted herself; and as far as she knew, she was unique.

There was still the question of the planet's strange silence. Now she had another reason, aside from curiosity, to find the planet's inhabitants. She owed them a telescope. Maybe she could distract herself by looking for the people who'd created the mirror that made her fall in love. Though it was a lot, sex wasn't everything.

She spun the mirror to stabilize it and tucked it into a new orbit, safely away from the other satellites and edge-on to the stellar wind. The wind would get to it in time, and it would begin to flutter and fold. That would take decades or maybe centuries. Meanwhile, the mirror would remain as it was: a silver disk, spinning rapidly around the planet's equator and its own center.

After she finished with the mirror, Big Green Mama stepped down to the planetary surface. En route she decreased her size, not wishing to crush anything. Life is rare and precious and always unique. All the Big Mamas are careful around it.

She landed on a beach of yellow sand. On one side of her, blue waves rolled in. On the other side, a green forest rippled in the wind. The air smelled of salt water and life. She took a deep, deep breath and exhaled. What an entrancing place! Perfect for a honeymoon! Thinking that, she began to look around.

Big Mamas can move quickly and don't need to go through intervening space, though they usually do, since time doesn't mean a lot to them. Why not take the long way and see everything? But Big Green Mama was curious and even worried. What could make a planet like this so quiet? The silence gave her the willies. She decided on short cuts. *Zap!* She vanished from the beach and reappeared on another part of the planetary surface.

All that day and into the night she zipped and zapped around the planet, looking for evidence of intelligent life. She found cities, but they were empty of people, their buildings partially fallen. She found highways, their concrete cracked and crumbling. The planet's rivers held broken locks and dams. There were silted-up harbors and long, straight depressions that might once have been canals. In some spots, she could look down on the land and see where fields had been, edged with windbreaks. Many of the windbreak trees were still standing, though old and twisted. Instead of crops, she saw wild vegetation.

Obviously, she was looking at the remains of a great, planet-wide civilization.

It had died recently. Given time, the satellites would have fallen from orbit and the cities vanished entirely. The ruination here looked like the work of a century or two. She had just barely missed the people of this world.

The thought made her sad and lonely, as well as horny. She was still haunted by her own reflection. Maybe if she'd found the planet's people, they would have taken her mind off her peculiar passion. But now, in the midst of desolation, her longing for company and sex grew more intense.

She ended at the beach where she had begun her journey. It was dawn, the planet's primary just beginning to rise over the wide ocean, touching the wave tops with light. A cool wind ruffled her hair. She walked along the beach, accompanied by her shadow. There was a solution to her problem, she realized. Big Mamas have many abilities; and one is binary fission. She could split herself in two and have the partner she wished for. But the process took a lot of energy. She would have to eat a big meal first.

The beach ended in a sand-filled harbor. No boats remained, but there were docks and breakwaters made of concrete with rusty pieces of rebar sticking out. She gathered the rebar, extracting it from the concrete like shellfish from a shell, and worked it between her fingers till the old metal was hot and soft. Then she stretched the rebar into thin wire and wove it into a net. Wading into the ocean, she cast the net. Out it went, shining like silver in the afternoon sunlight, splashed down, and sank from view. She pulled it in slowly, feeling the weight of something extra — fish, she hoped, though she didn't know anything about the planet's biology. Still, there were patterns in evolution, broad trends and similarities. As she lifted the net, she saw it held multitudes of long, narrow, silver-blue animals, which thrashed vigorously.

Fish or something close to fish. Big Green Mama said, "Yum!" She took a piece of rebar — she had some left — and quickly made it into a long, narrow knife. Crouching on the sandy beach, she killed the fish with quick compassion and cleaned them, one after another. They had a lot of spiny fins, but no scales. Their mouths were armed with beaks instead of teeth. Their skeletons looked odd to her, though she couldn't say how exactly. Something about the spine and ribs and skull. She had never filleted anything quite like them.

How did killing the fish fit with her earlier concern about life on the planet? Her concern was for species, not individuals.

Like all Big Mamas, she disliked unnecessary violence, but knew that the universe was not a kind place. Death came to everything, even the universe itself, which would someday either cool to darkness or crunch into a new beginning. Even the Big Mamas did not know which of these would happen, due to the difficulty in finding all the universe's matter and energy. The darn stuff hid itself, and tracking it down was more work than the Big Mamas wanted to do. The Big Poppas kept saying they would find the missing matter and energy, if it really existed. They hadn't yet.

Like all Big Mamas, Big Green Mama was a child of the universe and not always kind, though she tried to step softly among the stars and do more good than harm.

When she finished cleaning the fish, she built a fire of driftwood. Some of the fish she kept whole and roasted on sticks. Others she wrapped in seaweed and baked in coals. She ate deliberately, with grim determination, till her green belly bulged like a round mountain and she felt as if she never wanted to eat again.

After that, she stood up and stretched, her legs wide and her arms extended. Night had come, and the mirror she had left in orbit was rising: a line of brilliant light that lifted from the ocean's distant edge like an upright spear.

"Huh!" Big Green Mama grunted and began to divide. Soon, she was no longer able to stand. She fell into two pieces, which lay in the cool, dark, sand, both grunting. "Huh! Huh!"

The line of light at the horizon rose higher and higher. Reflections danced on the water. Big Green Mama kept grunting, as her two pieces filled out, each replacing whatever might be missing, slowly and painfully growing into two complete and separate women. At last, the process was done. The women lay side by side, both exhausted. By this time, the mirror was free of the horizon. The line of light hung at heaven's apex, like a horizontal spear or a fragment of a planetary ring.

"Well, that was difficult," said Big Green Mama.

"True enough," Big Green Mama replied.

"All's well that ends well," she told herself.

Her companion answered, "We don't know the ending yet."

Was she disagreeing with herself? Big Green Mama hoped not. At the moment, she was too tired to consider the problem. Closing her eyes, she drifted into a deep sleep.

She woke when the sun rose and rolled over. The place beside her was empty, though she could see the impression her companion had left in the sand.

Where? she wondered and sat up. Holy smoke, she was stiff and achy! The other Big Green Mama was in sight, wandering at the water's edge. The planet had no moon, except for the one she had just created, but there was a solar tide, and this was going out. The other Big Green Mama was searching through the shells and seaweed the receding water had left behind.

In what sense was the other Big Green Mama an "other," this Big Green Mama wondered. They were both daughters of the first Big Green Mama, identical to her and one another. Yet she, the Big Green Mama sitting in the sand, felt original and authentic. The person wandering down the beach seemed like a duplicate to her. How could this be? Her head began to hurt, and she decided not to think about the question.

The other Big Green Mama came back with a handful of lovely, empty shells. They had cold baked fish for breakfast.

Strangely enough, when she had another self to love, she felt less horny. Granted, the other Big Green Mama was handsome. She had never seen another person whose appearance she liked so much. But her admiration did not translate into lust. Instead, it was a dispassionate delight, the kind of emotion she felt when looking at an especially lovely nebula. Had the splitting done something to her libido? Or was her problem a sense of dispossession? She had been the only Big Green Mama in the universe. Now she was one of two. Granted, she had done this deliberately. Nonetheless, the result bothered her.

Time enough to worry about that later. For the moment, she wanted to find out what had happened to the people on this planet.

She explained this to her companion, who said, "I have already decided to solve the mystery here."

Of course she would say this. They were almost the same person.

"The best thing to do is to separate," the other Big Green Mama continued. "We can cover more ground and bother each other less. In addition, as we acquire new experiences, we will begin to become different people. I've always enjoyed my uniqueness. I assumed, when I decided to create you, that you would simply be more of me. Instead, you are a separate person with your own mind and will. This isn't what I wanted. To tell the truth, you give me the heebie-jeebies."

"I was about to say the same thing about you," Big Green Mama said.

They took off in different directions, going—zip! zap!—around the planet. Late in the afternoon, Big Green Mama found herself on a wide plain. Low plants rippled in the wind. An overgrown highway went straight east and west. Where it crossed a river, she found a broken bridge.

She settled there for the night, feeling lonely, though she wasn't sure what she was lonely for. The mirror rose again, a shining white line. She lay down and had disturbing dreams. When she woke, it was still dark. She ached all over. As she sat up, she noticed another person—a second self—lying next to her. Somehow, maybe out of longing, certainly without intending to, she had divided again. Big Green Mama cursed. Her other self woke. They examined one another by the light of the mirror and realized they were both smaller than the previous Big Green Mama and both very hungry.

Leaping up, they waded into the river, caught fish with their hands, and ate the animals raw. When they were full, they sat down to discuss the problem.

"We could separate, as we did before," Big Green Mama said. "But I'm afraid that loneliness would drive me to create another you. Therefore, I suggest we stay together. I suppose we can learn to like one another. I always used to like myself."

"I have an idea," said the other Big Green Mama. "It won't be hard for me to tweak some genes and make a few small adjustments to your anatomy. I can turn you into a Big Green Poppa. We would both remain the same person, but with one important difference, which would—I hope—enable us to tolerate each other and not become lonely."

"That's an excellent idea," said Big Green Mama. "Except for one small detail. I am perfectly happy being who I am. You're the one who should become a Big Green Poppa."

They argued back and forth, till the mirror set and the morning star appeared. (The planet had a companion world that was closer to its sun. It wasn't as bright as Venus in Big Green Mama's home planetary system, since it lacked the Venusian cloud cover. Still, it was easy to see in the planet's early morning sky.) At last, they decided to play paper, scissors, stone. Whoever won would remain a woman.

So they played: two handsome green women, sitting cross-legged on a bridge, facing one another. The wide plain stretched around them. Below them, shallow water ran through a sandy river bed. Animals with downy wings—rather like bats, though active in the daylight—fluttered over them, making barely audible noises.

Big Green Mama lost the game. "The best two out of the three," she pleaded.

"Like heck," her companion said. "We have a deal. You are going to become a Poppa."

Like all Big Mamas, these two were honorable gamblers, at least when they were playing one another. If necessary, when playing against a stranger, a Big Mama will cheat. Big Black Mama had done so, when she played Tentacle Man, a mean brute who wanted to eat her.

In this case, Big Green Mama was playing a relative—herself, in fact—and she had lost fair and square. After some more pleading and whining, she said, "Oh, very well."

They stood up, facing each other on the broken bridge. The other Mama reached out a big green hand. Tweak! tweak! she went. Push! Pull! In less than a minute, Big Green Mama's lovely round breasts were gone, and something new dangled between her legs.

"I don't think I'm going to like this," Big Green Poppa said.

"Nonsense! You look fine! Let me slim down those hips a bit and widen the waist." Big Green Mama did so.

Big Green Poppa grimaced. Then he noticed how very handsome the woman in front of him was. Neither of them had clothes on. He could see every wonderful millimeter of soft, green skin, every curl and tendril of lustrous hair. He noticed the slight tinge of pink in Big Green Mama's lips and in her nipples, as well. This was one heck of a lady! And somehow, after this most recent change, his libido had come back. His new member began to rise like the mirror he had put in the sky.

"You see," said Big Green Mama. "You do like what has happened."

They made love on the bridge, then went on together—zip! zap!—through the planet's empty cities. At sundown, they found themselves in a city on a hill. They arrived in a square at the city's center. Ruined towers rose around them. The climate was subtropical; and the local vines were as ferocious as kudzu on Earth. They wrapped the towers in foliage, so the materials beneath — brick, concrete and rusty metal — were barely visible. Trees grew in the streets, on balconies and rooftops.

Their arrival startled a flock of animals, which flew up, shrieking. Their downy wings shone white and pale pink in the late afternoon sunlight. Big Green Poppa watched them, noting the narrow tails, ending in tufts of feathers, and the long beaks or muzzles. On a bet, these last contained teeth. Aha, he thought. His new hormones were changing him. He hadn't been this analytic previously, or so interested in taxonomy.

There was a river in the city, which they found before nightfall. There wasn't time to catch fish. They camped on the bank, planning to go fishing in the morning, and made love before they went to sleep.

Big Green Poppa had disturbing dreams. When he woke, it was midnight. The mirror hung above him like a horizontal spear, and next to him — cuddled against his body — was another man.

What? he thought and sat up. The mirror was bright enough to show him what had happened. Both he and Big Green Mama had split. The result was four people, noticeably smaller than the previous two. He was hungry. No, he was voracious. His belly seemed like a black hole. He was afraid he might eat his companions.

The situation was getting serious. How often could this happen? Would he keep dividing until he was microscopic? Or was there some kind of lower limit? His cells had a set size, as far as he knew. As he grew smaller, the number of cells must be decreasing. At some point, there would be too few to make a person. He would diminish to death.

Maybe he could stave off this end by eating constantly, madly building the new cells he needed to survive. This didn't sound like much of a life. He was so hungry! He got up and walked through the dark streets. Above him, the mirror's bright line moved slowly toward the west.

Morning came finally. He went to the river and caught fish, barely pausing to kill them before he ate them, chewing the raw flesh eagerly, grinding the bones till they could do him no harm.

When he was finished, he went back to his companions. The man was entwined with one of the women. The other woman stood looking at the river. "We did it again," she said when Big Green Poppa approached. "Your clone seems interested in sex."

"So does your clone," Big Green Poppa replied.

"That leaves the thinking to us," Big Green Mama said. "Two questions occur to me about this planet. One is, what happened to the people? The other is, why are we dividing like bacteria?"

Big Green Poppa had no answer.

Their duplicates finished making love and were ravenous. This led to more fishing. The results were roasted. They sat around the fire and ate. Big Green Poppa stared at the other Big Green Poppa. His body was sleek and rounded, almost feminine in appearance. His green face had a smooth, sensual look—lips full and eyes heavy-lidded. This last might have been exhaustion, due to binary fission and sex.

Do I look like that? Big Green Poppa wondered. The duplicate's shoulders were wide, his waist narrow and his male equipment large, though quiescent at the moment. Maybe roughness and angularity were not necessary, Big Green Poppa told himself. Women were the default sex. He knew that, though he wasn't a scientist. Maybe it was okay to look a little feminine.

"This diet could become boring," said one of the Big Green Mamas finally. "What are we going to do?"

"I believe we should solve the mystery of this planet," the other Big Green Mama said. "I've never had trouble with binary fission before, and the only thing that's changed is my location."

"I don't remember doing it before," said the other Big Green Poppa.

"That's true," Big Green Mama admitted. "I haven't. But in theory it should be easy and not lead to the consequences we have experienced here."

"We'd better solve the mystery quickly," Big Green Mama said. "It seems likely or at least possible that we will divide every time we go to sleep. How many more of us do we want? How small can we get, before something eats us? Or steps on us?"

"Let's try sleeping in shifts," the other Big Green Poppa said. "The ones of us who remain awake can watch for signs of binary fission. If it seems to be starting, we will wake the person in question."

"Or we could leave the planet," Big Green Poppa said. "If it's the cause of our problem, the problem may end once we are back in space."

They considered this plan. Finally, Big Green Mama said, "If the problem is sleeping, let's sleep in space or on the next planet out. I looked at it on my way into the system. It may be habitable. In any case, it will be more comfortable than sleeping on the bare slope of a gravity well."

They spent the rest of the day exploring the planet they were on, finding more ruins and no signs of living people. At sundown, they climbed into space and walked up the long, gentle gravity slope that led to the next planet out.

From above, it looked far less pleasant than the world they had just left. But there was water: a pair of shallow oceans and lots of river beds, though most of these last were dry. The oceans and polar caps were edged with blue-green vegetation. Most of the rest of the world looked bare and brown, except for the high mountains. There were some spectacular volcanoes, though none equal to those on Mars. These were capped with snow and had faint, blue-green steaks on their lower slopes.

"Well," said Big Green Mama, looking down. "It's big enough to hold an atmosphere with water, and the mountains suggest some tectonic activity. A live planet in both senses. Let's go down."

They did, landing by one of the oceans. In the distance four shield volcanoes rose, small enough to be visible as mountains, but large enough to be impressive. All were snowcapped. One was smoking slightly.

"A live world," said Big Green Mama with satisfaction.

Low plants covered the ground around them. They looked like lichens or mosses. Here and there, stalks rose, a meter tall at most, leafless and blue-green. Were these for reproduction? Or were the Mamas and Poppas thinking about sex too much? Water lay maybe ten meters to the north of them: a wide, silver expanse that shone in dim sunlight. Looking up, they saw the planet's primary, high and small, surrounded by cirrus clouds. Even this close to an ocean, the air seemed desert-like, cold and dry.

There was no driftwood. They could not build a fire. Instead, they huddled together, keeping one another warm. The sun went down. Somehow—due to fatigue from the long climb up from the inner planet or simple careless-ness—they did not set a watch. When they woke, there were eight of them, all smaller than the previous four.

"This is becoming positively Malthusian," said one of the Big Green Mamas in a tone of anger. "And I don't like it one little bit."

"Little is right," said Big Green Poppa, looking around and thinking he might have to change his name. They were all still intensely green: like grass, midsummer foliage, and forest rivers running in the shadows of trees.

"Well," said another Big Green Poppa. "We have elimi-nated one theory. The binary fission is not caused by the planet we just left."

"That isn't correct," a third Big Green Poppa said. "The planet may have begun a process, which can continue elsewhere."

"I'm hungry," a Big Green Mama said. "And I don't think there's anything to eat on the planet."

"We are drawing conclusions in the absence of data," said a Big Green Poppa. "Let's walk along the shore and look for food. If we find none, we can head back down to the previous planet."

"I'm so tired of fish," said a Big Green Mama.

"Don't whine," said a Poppa. "It isn't becoming in a be-ing as powerful as we are."

"Powerful, heck!" said a Mama. "Look at us! We're fall-ing into pieces."

"Only eight so far," said a Poppa.

Arguing and complaining, they got up and walked along the beach. It was made of coarse, brown sand, damp along the water's edge. Objects lay there: tendrils of marine weed and shells the size of a fingernail. A few animals crawled through the debris, multi-legged and no bigger than the shells.

At length, they saw something ahead of them: a dome—no, a series of domes, made of glass and gleaming in the dim sunlight. They rose like so many beach houses between sand and blue-green vegetation.

This made them pick up their pace. In almost no time, they were at the domes. Close up, they saw that the glass was pitted and opaque. But it seemed to be solid. Each dome had a door, which looked to be an airlock.

"The people here—if they are still here—aren't native to this planet," said a Big Green Mama.

"Most likely they come from the planet we just left," said a Big Green Poppa.

"Well, knock," said someone else. "I want breakfast and an explanation, if that is possible."

A Big Green Mama knocked.

For a while, nothing happened. The eight green people fidgeted. Finally, when they were ready to do some more knocking, a lot louder this time, the airlock opened. A person stepped out. It wore an atmosphere suit. Nonetheless, they could tell something about its gross anatomy. Four legs supported a long body. At one end, which seemed to be the front end, was a torso with two arms and a head. The legs were short and thick, the arms long and narrow. It wasn't possible to tell much about the head, which was encased in a helmet. But there was a transparent front piece.

Looking in, they saw a broad, pink, scaly face. The creature had two large, yellow eyes with vertical slit pupils, no visible nose and a wide, lipless mouth.

"Hardly pretty," said a Big Green Mama.

"But brave," said a Poppa. "It isn't flinching, though we must look strange to it."

"I suppose we're going to have to learn its language," said a Mama with a sigh. "It better be a quick procedure, or we will become as numerous as ants and not much bigger."

"And maybe not much smarter," said another Mama. "It's easy to fool an ant."[1]

The person opened something that looked like a metal folder. Inside was a pair of screens, which lit up. One showed a diagram of the planetary system they were in. The other showed a drawing that was almost certainly a member of the same species as the person in front of them: stocky and short-legged with two long, thin arms and a bulbous, hairless head.

The person pointed at the picture of the centaur. "Skwork," it said clearly. "Skwork."

Well, that wasn't so difficult. The person or its species was named Skwork. In a matter of minutes, they had learned that this planet was named Fleeb. The next planet in was Twil. Skwork or the skwork had come from Twil to Fleeb.

Numbers came next and were easy. They learned that the Skwork had come to Fleeb three centuries previously.

....

1 This last is a quote from E.O. Wilson, who knows what he's talking about when it comes to ants. How was Big Green Mama able to quote Wilson? As a group, Big Mamas and Poppas have a lot of information, though it is not usually well organized. They are autodidacts and not scientifically trained.

This was interesting, but it was past lunchtime. It was possible to draw on the screens, using a stylus. One of the Big Green Mamas drew a request for food.

The person spoke, though not to them. They could hear its voice through the suit and the thin air. They waited, hoping they had heard a request for lunch. After a while, the airlock opened, and a cart trundled out. The person opened the cart. There were containers inside. The person handed these around.

Food! Steaming gray mush! Cold water! Crisp and bitter crackers! They gobbled everything down.

The person watched them with obvious surprise. They must look very hungry. After they were done, the cart trundled back inside. The person reopened its folder. It gestured at the Mamas and Poppas, then at the dark-blue sky, and finally at the diagram of the planetary system. That seemed clear enough. The person was asking where they had come from.

A Big Green Mama pointed at Twil in the diagram.

The person's head jerked up, and it took several steps back. Its free hand made a warding motion. Stay back, the motion seemed to say. Or else, go away.

The green people looked at one another. What had they done?

The person shifted back and forth from foot to foot. Clearly, it was distressed. It spoke urgently within its suit. A conversation was going on, possibly an argument. The person's voice sounded loud and sharp.

The green people waited, not knowing what else to do.

Finally, the person closed its folder, putting the thing in a suit pocket. Then it gestured. Come along, this gesture told them.

They followed it away from the domes.

They walked for some time over blue-green vegetation. The land rose. There were outcroppings of dark, rough, igneous stone. At first, these were isolated lumps and chunks of rock. Then they came to ledges and low cliffs. Finally they reached a cliff with an opening: a volcanic tube. The person took out a rod. Light shone from one end. Follow me, the person said with a gesture. They entered the tube, the person leading, its light shining on dark, rough walls. The green people followed, keeping together, though they weren't afraid. Little can harm a Mama or Poppa, except large, mythological monsters and world-historical trends.

After they had gone some distance into the tube, a voice spoke ahead of them in a language they could understand. "What are you doing here? I told you not to bother me. You got yourselves into this mess. It's for you to handle the consequences."

Their guide stopped for a moment, then continued. They followed. Shortly thereafter, the tube ended. They entered a large spherical cave, its walls obviously volcanic. Dry vegetation lay in the middle of a curving floor, forming a primitive bed. A large—very large—pink person lay on the bed. As they entered the room, it lifted its head. Light reflected off pale yellow eyes. The person struggled onto four feet, moving slowly and with difficulty. It didn't look healthy, Big Green Poppa thought, though its color was handsome enough.

Bright pink, hairless skin covered its head and long, thin arms. The skin darkened as it went down the being's torso, turning to a deep rose-red. The darkening continued over the being's long back; and its rump was a rich burgundy. The stubby legs were striped pink and red.

The legs ended in feet with two wide toes. The arms ended in hands with three long fingers and a blunt opposable thumb. Like their guide, this person had no nose and a wide, lipless mouth. Where humans would have had ears, it had clusters of things like short, soft, fluffy feathers. These might be organs for hearing or smelling. Or they might be ornamental. They were certainly pretty.

The being glanced at them. "I believe I know what you are. I am a Skwork Large Parent."

This explained why they could understand the being. Big Mamas and Poppas always understood each other, even when they belonged to different species. As physicists tell us, at bottom—under the froth and details—the universe is uniform. Although the Mamas and Poppas seem to skip lightly over the surface of reality, they have the deepest of deep roots.

"I can't be called a Mama or Poppa, because the skwork are hermaphroditic and can in a pinch self fertilize, though this is not encouraged."

How? wondered Big Green Poppa. He could see no sex organs. Maybe they were hidden under the round belly or between the stocky legs.

"However, I serve the same purpose for the skwork as you do for your species. At present, I am in poor health, because my people are barely surviving and cannot return to their home planet. This is a poor place for them and me. What are you doing here? And why are there so many of you?"

Eagerly, with many interruptions, the green people explained. The Skwork Large Parent listened carefully. Their guide remained motionless, shining its light on all of them. In all likelihood, it did not understand anything they said.

At length they all wound down. After several moments of silence, the Skwork Large Parent spoke. "I believe I know what happened to you. In order to explain, I must tell you a story." It paused briefly and began.

Like many intelligent species, the skwork had fought wars; and as they became more civilized and more technologically adept, the wars became more horrific. A century and a half previously, they had reached their height of knowledge and power. At this point, after reaching space and colonizing Fleeb, they had a final war, using biological weapons. All four sides were armed with biotechnology, which they valued because it could be closely targeted. People died, not animals or plants. The infrastructure of civilization remained. One could simply march in and start up the machines abandoned by dying enemies. Their empty cities would become new homes for citizens of the triumphant country. What could be tidier or more ecologically responsible?

Corpses were a problem. It was unhealthy, even dangerous, to leave millions of dead bodies lying around. Scientists devised microbes that broke bodies apart quickly, reducing them to nontoxic byproducts, an organic slush that returned to the soil and fertilized it. Even bones dissolved, leaving nothing that might breed wild diseases or provide a home for the smart bugs they were using as weapons.

In theory, each nation's native population was immunized and safe from their own smart bugs. For the most part, this was true. However, there were four nations fighting; and it did not prove possible for each to protect its population against all the enemy bugs.

In time, a new problem emerged. The skwork weapons, their smart bugs, began to exchange genetic material. One cannot train a microbe to be patriotic. They have always survived by exchanging genes, not only with members of the same species, but with very different organisms. This is why they are so successful and remain the most numerous and varied life forms on every planet.

The skwork, who believed the key to history was competition, underestimated the extent to which their weapons could and would cooperate. The result was new diseases, with a wide range of lethal traits, omni-drug-resistant and changing so quickly that vaccines and antibiotics could not keep up.

When the skwork realized how dangerous the situation was, they tried to make peace — which they could do with one another, but not with the microbes. Just as they could not understand concepts such as patriotism, the microbes could not understand making peace with organisms they had previously killed. Given time, they might have adjusted. Microbes do, in time, become non-lethal parasites or even symbiotes. But there wasn't enough time. At the end of a century, the population of the skwork home world was dead. Only this colony survived, which had grown to a hundred thousand people. They no longer had space travel. Even if they did, they would be afraid to return to Twil. Most of the smart bugs had been designed to self-destruct. But some produced spores, which could remain in the soil for centuries or millennia, inactive until new victims appeared.

"This is why your guide was so upset, when he/she realized that you came from Twil. You are almost certainly infected. I suspect that infection is the reason that you have been dividing, though I don't understand the exact details. Maybe you have picked up the bugs that used to break down skwork bodies. In your case, because you are Big Mamas and Poppas, they aren't able to turn you into slush, but they have managed to compromise your integrity, so you are breaking apart, though in a very odd away.

"Or else you have picked up a virus that does something unexpected to cell division. That, after all, is the way that viruses replicate, by hijacking ordinary mitosis. In your case, instead of your cells individually dividing, your entire bodies divide.

"It is also possible that you are replicating because Twil is empty, and nature abhors a vacuum."

"No, it doesn't," a Big Green Mama said. "The universe is mostly empty. It's a natural condition."

The Skwork Large Parent said, "You are forgetting that vacuums are not really empty, but rather full of a foam made of particles, continuously coming into existence, then vanishing."

"Well, yes," said another Big Green Mama. "You might say that, and it might be true. But we are not particles. Different rules apply on a macro scale, which is where you and I exist. Up here, the universe is mostly empty."

"This is a pointless discussion about abstract ideas," said a Big Green Poppa. "We and our problem exist in a world that is real and solid. Thus I refute all of you." He kicked a stone on the cave's floor. Since he was not wearing shoes, he stubbed his big toe badly and hopped around for several moments saying, "Ow! Ow!"

As soon as he stopped hopping, another Big Green Poppa spoke up. "Why does the division only happen when we sleep?"

"You have a lot of strength of character," answered the Skwork Large Parent. "All Big Mamas and Poppas do. When you are awake, you can prevent the process. But not when you sleep."

The Big Mamas and Poppas all frowned, considering this idea doubtfully.

"Or maybe there is another explanation, which doesn't occur to me," the Skwork Large Parent added.

"What are we going to do?" a Big Green Poppa asked. "I don't want to keep dividing."

"I thought I would like another me," a Big Green Mama said. "But now I realize I want to exist in solitary splendor."

"And so do I," another Mama said.

"And I! And I! And I!" said all the others.

The Skwork Large Parent frowned. "We have two problems, then. No, three. How can we stop you from dividing further? What can we do about the numbers of you that exist already? And how can we save my people, the skwork?"

Everyone in the cave stood in silence, frowning deeply and trying to think.

Finally, a Big Green Mama said, "We know that humans have Big Mamas and Poppas, and we have just found out that the skwork have Large Parents. Is it possible that all living creatures have comparable beings? Is there a Big Microbe? Could it help us? How would we find it?"

"Not here," said the Skwork Large Parent. "If such a being exists, it is on Twil."

The Mamas and Poppas looked at one another and nodded.

"Thank you," said a Big Green Mama. "We will come back and tell you what we find on Twil, if we succeed in finding anything, and if you are still alive."

The Skwork Large Parent nodded wearily. The Mamas and Poppas left.

Down they went, along the gentle slope of the system's gravity well. The warm, yellow sun shone like a campfire. Bits of interplanetary debris flew past them like gnats.

All Mamas and Poppas are happiest when there's a problem to solve. A Poppa began to sing an old camping song from the early days of the universe.

> One hundred theoretical particles on the wall,
> One hundred theoretical particles.
> If one of those particles should happen to fall —
> Ninety-nine theoretical particles on the wall.[2]

The other Poppas and Mamas joined in. They sang lustily till they reached Twil, then dropped out of the sky, landing lightly on the planet's surface.

"What now?" asked a Big Green Poppa. "How does one find a microbe?"

"They are everywhere, you fool," replied another Poppa. "The problem is finding the right one."

They tried shouting. "Hey, Big Microbe! Where are you? Yo! Are you there?"

Nothing answered them, except the wind.

....

2 You may ask (a) how could there be a wall at the beginning of the universe, and (b) how could theoretical particles adhere to it? The Mamas and Poppas would reply, (a) the wall is the wall around the universe; back then it was close and easy to see; and (b) one of the particles' theoretical properties was "stickiness," an early form of entanglement.

"Maybe the Big Microbe is in some other place," a Big Mama said finally. "Maybe we ought to split up and go looking for it."

The others winced at the word "split." But in the end, they did divide into pairs—one Mama and one Poppa—and went zipping and zapping around the planet. At every stop, they called, "Yo! Big Microbe!"

Only one pair got an answer, and it wasn't from the Big Microbe. Instead, it came from the other Big Green Mama, the one who'd been left on the beach when their adventure began. She had traveled south and ended in a vast tropical city, full of wild fruit trees. A river ran through the city, full of fish. There—or maybe along the way—she had turned into sixteen Mamas, all of them smaller and paler than the original.

"I was hoping you'd find me," they said. "That's why I picked this vast ruined city. I thought it might draw you. Mamas and Poppas are usually interested in civilization, and a ruined civilization is like a scab. One has to pick at it. Also, there is enough to eat here. But we are afraid to sleep."

"This is getting serious," the Big Poppa said. "There seems no end to our proliferation, and I don't like what we're becoming."

"Thanks a lot!" said the little, pale Mamas.

"You'd better come with us," the Big Mama said; and they rejoined the others. Everyone exclaimed over the little, pale Mamas. Then the other returning pairs confessed failure. No one had found the Big Microbe, though they had called loudly in many places.

A Green Poppa said, "I'm starting to think that microbes cannot hear."

"You may be right," said a Mama. "I've never seen a microbe with ears. But some kinds are heliotropic. What if we increase the radiation put out by the planet's star? That might draw the Big Microbe from wherever it may be hiding."

"Too much work," said a Poppa. "And too drastic. What if we botched the job? The star might blow up. What a mess that would be! But your idea reminds me that some microbes are thermophilic. Instead of increasing the light put out by the planet's star, we could increase the planet's level of volcanism. It would only require poking a few holes in the planet's crust. That might attract the Big Microbe's attention, and it would be far easier than turning up a star."

"It would still be destructive," another Poppa objected. "What if we poked too deeply? We might flood entire regions with lava! Remember the Deccan Flats!"

All the Mamas and Poppas, big and little, nodded somberly, remembering an event that had been planned as fireworks for a party. A fine mess it had turned out to be!

"What if the volcanoes we created threw so much ash into the atmosphere that the planet suddenly cooled?" the Poppa continued. "We could create an ice age! And if the Big Microbe is thermophilic, that would certainly drive it away."

"Let's try something more subtle. There are microbes that are sensitive to magnetism. What if we alter the planet's magnetic field? Strengthen it? Or weaken it? Flip it entirely over?"

"What about chemistry?" asked a Mama. "There are a thousand things we could do to the planet's chemistry, which would attract the attention of microbes living here."

"*And cause them to die,*" said a whispery voice behind them.

They all turned and stared at an oval that stood—if that was the right word for a thing without legs—on the surface vegetation. Five meters tall, it was translucent and faintly green. Dark objects were visible inside it. Organs? wondered the Mamas and Poppas. Or organelles? What exactly was an organelle?[3]

The oval's surface was covered with fine hairs that waved gently, as if in a mild wind, though no wind was blowing. "*I am the Big Microbe,*" it said, speaking without a mouth. "*My single-celled people are the most successful of organisms, living in water, soil, air, deep cracks far under the planet's surface, by boiling vents in the black depths of the ocean, within plants and animals. They thrive in heat and cold, light and dark, oxygen and lack of oxygen. Every age is the Age of Microbes!*"

"Er, yes," said a Big Green Mama, acutely aware that the Microbe was taller than she. She tried edging up to a greater height, but the Microbe matched her, flowing easily toward the sky. "How can you hear us, without ears?" asked a Poppa. "And how can we hear you? Are you telepathic? Are we?"

"*I'm not telepathic; but I am sensitive to light, heat, magnetism, pressure, and many chemicals. This enables me to understand the signals you send out, though I don't have ears and don't know your language. I have no idea how you are able to understand me. Now to the important question...*" The Microbe expanded, becoming taller and broader. The hairs that covered it vibrated excitedly. The dark spots inside rolled like angry eyes. "*Who are you, and why do you want to change my people's planet?*"

....

3 A membrane-bound structure that performs a specific function within a cell: a "little organ." Prokaryotes, such as bacteria and blue-green algae, do not usually have organelles. Eukaryotes do by definition.

The Mamas and Poppas tried to explain, all talking at once. It was the dividing, the Skwork Large Parent, fear of death…

"*You want to kill my people, because you are afraid of death. Is that what you are trying to say?*"

"Not exactly," the Mamas and Poppas said.

"*Death is the fate of all multi-celled creatures. My people alone are immortal, dividing endlessly and replicating themselves forever, unless they are killed by the likes of you. Even then, their spores may survive. They are remarkably durable. Some have traveled through space and established life on other planets. Some have produced living organisms after a million years or more.*" The Big Microbe paused and appeared to be brooding, insofar as a ten-meter-tall blob of cytoplasm can be said to brood. "*Though it is not clear to me that the creatures created by fission or spores are the same as their originals. The offspring (or dividends) begin with genetic identity, but how long does that last? Time, experience, mutation, and exchanges with other organisms change us all. We are none of us the beings we began to be.*"

"Well, yes," put in a Big Green Poppa. "But we are desperate at the moment and in no mood for philosophy. Can you help us with our problem?"

"No," said the Big Microbe. "*It's obvious that you have been infected by something that has invaded your genetic material and twisted it toward a new purpose*"

"Knickers in a knot," muttered a Poppa and was shushed by the rest.

"*Perhaps this happened during your first division, the one you planned. Binary fission is hard work, and one is vulnerable until the task is complete.*

"*It wasn't one of my people who infected you, nor was it a prion, which is lucky for you. The Big Prion is a seriously weird being. I suspect the cause of your problem is a virus, and therefore you need to talk to the Big Virus.*"

The Mamas and Poppas exclaimed in dismay. How could they find a virus?

"*They are everywhere,*" the Big Microbe replied. "*No organism escapes them. They occupy every plant, animal, and microbe. They are the perfect parasites, stripped of everything except the ability to prey, using all of us for their own purposes. There are even viruses in ME!*" As the Microbe spoke, it grew larger, rising toward the sky and spreading from side to side. An alarming sight, they thought, until they noticed the Microbe was thinning as it spread. Its green body grew colorless and transparent. The spots inside it — organelles — grew dim and difficult to see, except for one spot more or less in the Microbe's middle. This grew larger and more distinct. They leaned forward, peering. It was a sphere, with spines sticking out all over.

Nasty, the Mamas and Poppas thought.

The Microbe had become a cloud, floating between earth and heaven. A mild wind tugged at it, making its edges flutter and tearing off little shreds. It was coming apart, they realized.

The thing inside grew darker, firmer, and solider. They could see the spines clearly now. Some ended in points, others in hooks. This had to be a predator. As they thought this, the Big Microbe vanished. The sphere remained, its hard shell gleaming in the sun.

"*I KNOW YOU, BECAUSE YOU ARE FULL OF MY PEOPLE. HALF YOUR GENETIC MATERIAL IS MY FOLK, WHO HAVE INSERTED THEMSELVES*

INTO YOUR DNA AND RNA. JUNK, YOU CALL US CONTEMPTUOUSLY. BUT WE ARE NOT!

"DON'T THINK YOU CAN HIDE YOUR THOUGHTS FROM ME! AND DON'T THINK BAD THINGS ABOUT ME OR MY PEOPLE! REMEMBER THAT YOU EXIST TO PROVIDE US WITH THE ABILITY TO REPLICATE. THE MICROBES CAME FIRST. MULTI-CELLED CREATURES CAME AFTER. BUT WE ARE THE TOP OF THE FOOD CHAIN!"

The being's voice echoed triumphantly in their minds. It began to rotate in (they surmised) a slow dance of victory and pride.

"Can you help us?" as especially courageous Poppa asked.

The Virus stopped moving. *"HELP? WHY SHOULD I HELP ANYONE?"*

The Mamas and Poppas looked at one another, puzzled. How does one reason with a predator or parasite? For a while, no one spoke. The Big Virus resumed its dance, sunlight flashing off its points and hooks.

Finally a Big Green Mama said, "You may be at the top of the food chain. But you need the food chain. Many of your people can't survive, unless they are safely lodged inside a host; and none can reproduce without a host."

"SO WHAT? THE UNIVERSE IF FULL OF HOSTS!"

"Your people on this planet rely on the hosts here."

"SO WHAT? THE PLANET HAS PLENTY OF HOSTS."

"Didn't you lose people when the skwork on this planet died?'

The Virus stopped turning. "*A FEW*," it said after a momentary hesitation. "*THEY WERE SPECIALIZED AND COULD NOT MOVE TO ANOTHER HOST. MY PEOPLE ARE NUMEROUS. WE CAN AFFORD TO LOSE A FEW OF US.*"

"An efficient predator doesn't kill all its prey. An efficient parasite leaves its host alive," said the Mama.

"*MY PEOPLE DIDN'T KILL THEIR PREY. THE PREY KILLED ONE ANOTHER!*"

"No matter who did the deed, your people are gone."

"*ONLY A FEW!*"

"What if this planet died? If you are like other Big Beings, then you are local to this system. Other Big Viruses care for the viruses in other systems."

"*MAYBE*," said the Virus grudgingly. "*BUT THIS PLANET ISN'T GOING TO DIE IN THE NEAR FUTURE. WHEN IT DOES, WE WILL TRAVEL AWAY…*" The Virus's voice trailed off.

"In what?' asked the Mama. "The last of the skwork are dying. They won't be around to carry your people to the stars."

"*HOW DARE THEY BE SO UNCARING? THEY SHOULD HAVE PRESERVED THEMSELVES!*" The Virus bounced up and down in an agitated fashion. Then its motion slowed. "*WE COULD TRAVEL IN YOU. YOU ARE CLEARLY STAR-FARING.*"

"We are dividing and redividing, growing smaller and smaller. We think our abilities are diminishing as we diminish. Soon we may not be able to travel among the stars."

"*GO NOW!*"

"So far as we know, we are carrying only one virus, the one that makes us divide. We might be able to carry it a brief distance, before we perish. But what about the rest of your people? And you?"

The Big Virus spun so rapidly that they couldn't make out any details of structure. There was only motion and flickering sunlight. Suddenly it stopped. "WHY AM I WORRYING? THIS PLANET IS GOOD FOR BILLIONS OF YEARS. SOMETHING WILL TURN UP BEFORE THE PLANET DIES."

"Our powers are diminishing," a Big Poppa said. "They are not yet gone. We can destroy this planet."

"WHY WOULD YOU DO THAT?"

"Why not?" asked another Poppa.

A Mama added, "Some of your people may survive on the next planet out, though it has an impoverished ecological system and will never provide the range of hosts you have here."

"We may destroy that planet as well," a Poppa added in a friendly, helpful tone.

"YOU ARE MONSTERS!" the Virus cried.

The Mamas and Poppas folded their green arms. Several tapped green feet against the surface vegetation.

"Don't whine," said a Mama. "It's unbecoming, even in a virus."

"We are merely showing you where indifference to others leads," a Poppa added.

"Now," said another Mama. "Can you help us? We promise to leave this system intact, if you help us stop dividing."

The Big Virus bobbed up and down, obviously thinking, though it was strange to think of a virus thinking. Still, all Big Beings had unusual abilities, as the Big Mamas and Poppas knew.

At last, the Virus spoke. "*YOU ARE RIGHT. AN EFFICIENT PARASITE DOES NOT DESTROY ITS HOST, AND THOSE WHO ARE AT THE TOP OF THE FOOD CHAIN NEED THE REST OF THE FOOD CHAIN. IN THIS, ALTHOUGH WE ARE THE BEST AND MOST ECONOMICAL OF BEINGS, WE MAY BE SAID TO BE MORE VULNERABLE THAN THOSE MISERABLE MICROBES. MANY OF THEM NEED NOTHING EXCEPT A FEW MINERALS AND A SOURCE OF ENERGY. THE WRETCHED CHEATS!*"

"You are whining again," said a Mama.

"*I WILL HELP YOU, IN SPITE OF YOUR CRITICISM,*" the Virus said. "*LINE UP. I NEED TO EXAMINE YOU AND FIND OUT WHICH OF MY PEOPLE HAS INFECTED YOU.*"

A suspicious Poppa muttered, "What if it isn't being honest? Only a fool would trust a virus. Some of us need to stand off to the side and watch."

"If you wish," a Mama said.

Several of the Big Green People, most of them male, moved off to the side. Everyone else lined up. The Big Virus went down the line, probing with superfine spines that slid in the Green People's flesh like acupuncture needles. "*HMMMMMM,*" it said.

The Green People quivered.

Finally it added, "*I HAVE FOUND THE SOURCE OF YOUR PROBLEM. IT IS A VIRUS THAT NORMALLY INFECTS MICROBES AND USES, EVEN ENCOURAGES, THEIR FISSION IN ORDER TO MULTIPLY ITSELF. I WILL NOW CREATE A NEW*

VIRUS, WHICH WILL INFECT YOU AND DISABLE THE ORIGINAL INFECTION. ARE YOU READY?"

The Green People shifted from one foot to the other. "Er, yes."

"*WATCH ME CLOSELY,*" said the Virus. "*THIS IS ONE HECK OF A TRICK. THERE IS NOTHING ON MY HOOKS OR UP MY SPINES. PRESTO! MAGICO!*"

The Big Virus crumbled into a cloud of glittering dust, which whirled in the wind, enveloping all the Big People, even those who were standing off to one side.

"What the heck!" cried a Big Poppa.

They all began to sneeze. These were not the kind of small, refined sneezes that a cat produces. Instead, they were large and full-bodied "achoos!" that went on and on. Some Mamas and Poppas ended bent over. Others ended on their knees, gasping for breath between each gigantic sneeze. They couldn't speak, but they could think, though not especially well. Betrayed, they thought.

At last the sneezing quieted. They straightened up or stood and wiped their noses. What had that been about? Were they all right now? Or had the Big Virus infected them? And with what?

"Never trust a virus," a Poppa said.

"They are part of the web of life," countered a Mama. "Though they may not be alive, according to some definitions. Still, they infect life and change it. I see no reason they should be more unreliable than life in general."

"Maybe," the Poppa said and looked at his hands, afraid they might be changing. No, they were as big and green and handsome as always, except for the bitten nails. He had begun biting his nails on Fleeb. What an adventure this had been. He would never fall in love with himself again.

If he had a future. For all he knew, he might keep dividing until he reached the size of a microbe or a subatomic particle. He imagined himself as an electron in a Big Green Atom, whizzing in a cloud of his other male selves around a nucleus of infinitesimal Mamas. Oh, it was painful to contemplate! He sighed and glanced around at the rest of him. All the Mamas and Poppas looked worn-out and discouraged.

"We might as well go fishing," a Mama said finally. "We will find out tomorrow if the Big Virus has cured us of division. Either there will be more of us, or there won't. In the meantime, we need to eat."

The others nodded. They went to find a beach.

The beach they found was fine black sand that glittered in the tropical sun. One side was edged with blue waves, the other side with forest. The trees had tall, straight trunks and loose bark that hung down in loops and long strings, rather like eucalyptus trees, though the scent was not the least bit similar. Large, ragged leaves grew in clusters atop each trunk, rather like palm trees, except for the copper-red color.

They gathered bark and twisted it into strong cord, then knotted the cord into nets. Then they went fishing. Afterward, they had a bake on the beach. The sun went down amid scarlet clouds. The mirror rose like a spear. They finished eating and sat around the fire, singing and telling stories—less for pleasure than out of fear. What would happen if they went to sleep?

Even Mamas and Poppas have their limits. One by one, they fell silent and began to doze. At length, there was no sound except the fire snapping and some hearty snores.

They woke when sunlight slanted through the copper-leafed forest, rose quickly, and counted themselves. They had not multiplied overnight.

"Cured," cried a Poppa in relief.

"There are still too many of us," replied a Mama. "Twenty-four! Of varying sexes and sizes! I want to go back to the person I was, single and unique."

"You'll have to take that up with the Big Virus," said another Big Mama.

They tried. They really tried, wandering the planet for days, yelling, "Yo, Big Virus!" in choked voices, because they all had terrible colds.

But the Big Virus never reappeared, maybe because it was inside them, ready to be carried to the stars. They considered that possibility now and then, imaging the BV's genetic material free of its spiny shell, infiltrating their bodies and weaving itself into their DNA and RNA. A creepy idea. Maybe they should ignore it. The colds cleared up after a week. They all felt fine.

At last they gathered together for a consultation.

"I think we are stuck in this condition," a Mama said. "I suggest we leave this planet and take off in different directions. Then we will each be unique again. Frankly, if I never see any of you again, it will be soon enough."

"That sounds like a good idea," said a Poppa. "While we are traveling in solitary splendor, we should look for star-faring civilizations and tell them about the skwork. The remnants of this unhappy species need to be rescued. I don't think we can do it. Our grasp of biotechnology is not adequate, and who can say what diseases we may carry still?"

They nodded and shook hands, and all departed, leaping into the sky and climbing the gravity slope that led from the system's star. Did any of them pay the promised visit to the Skwork Large Parent? No, because they weren't sure who had made the promise. Who were any of them, at the moment? Not the original Big Green Mama, although they were genetically identical to her.[4] We are all more than our genes, and our DNA contains much that isn't us.

Instead, it can—and should—be argued that we are complex products of time and experience, change and growth, the interaction of DNA and cellular machinery and the environment and who can say what else? It's a process that doesn't end, until we end.

The Mamas and Poppas did not have opinions on this topic, not being biologists or science fiction writers. They simply knew that they had to get away from each other. Each of them promised him- or herself to value difference in the future and never fall into self-love again, or underestimate a microbe or a virus.

Note: We know from other stories that the Big Mamas and Poppas can travel in time. Why didn't one or several of them go back and tell the original Big Green Mama to not divide? The answer is obvious. If they did this, they would vanish, having never existed. It was a

4 Except for whatever the Big Virus might have done to their DNA and whatever other changes might have occurred already.

form of suicide, and all Big Mamas and Poppas are firmly opposed to every form of self-
destruction.

BIG RED MAMA IN TIME
AND MORRIS, MINNESOTA

One morning Big Red Mama was walking along, enjoying the fine, warm Cretaceous mud as it oozed up between her bare, red toes. As she lifted each foot, the mud sucked at the sole. She enjoyed this as well. She was a woman in love with sensation of every kind; although, as a rule, she preferred pleasant sensations, such as warm mud or the wind that currently blew around her, flipping her hair, which was as black as coal, as straight as rain, and as long as an afternoon in a small Midwestern town on Sunday in the nineteenth century.

She thanked fate and her abilities that she was in the Cretaceous and not in a small Midwestern town in the nineteenth century. Among other dislikable things, such towns were full of people who did not like Indians.

The wind was blowing off the ocean and smelled of salt water, seaweed, and fish. A pleasant odor, in her opinion. It reminded her of plesiosaurs lifting their long, narrow necks from the water; pterosaurs gliding on long, wide wings; enormous sharks; and marine crocodiles with flippers instead of feet.

What a fine place to be! A time without Sunday or any other kind of day, except sunny, cloudy, and rainy. The temperature was always temperate. The fauna had not evolved as far as prejudice. She frightened some of them, and others thought she looked tasty; but that wasn't prejudice, and she could handle it. Easier to face down a T Rex than a narrow-eyed bigot.[1]

She turned a corner around a clump of cycads. There, on the ground, in the oozing mud, was a therapod dinosaur. Big Red Mama was not a taxonomist, and she wasn't sure what kind of therapod it was. Not one of the little ones. It had to be more than five meters long, large enough so it didn't need feathers for insulation, but it clearly came from a feathered ancestry. A crest of dark, hair-like down ran along its spine, and its long tail ended in a hairy tuft. Most likely, these were decorative remnants, used for identification or courting display, though the tuft might also be useful in dealing with flies. The animal's back was reddish brown with black stripes. The belly was pale tan. The forepaws and feet had large, dangerous-looking claws. She couldn't tell anything about the head, because it was gone, neatly cut off at the neck.

What the heck? thought Big Red Mama. Nothing in this age made a cut that neat; and what kind of fool animal would take the head, which was mostly bone, instead of tearing off a leg or ripping into the round, fat belly?

This was an easy question to answer. Her lovely refuge had been invaded by intelligent life. She glared at the ground, looking for signs of the killer. There they were: boot prints, pressed deeply into the mud. There was no

....

1 This is not BS. Big Red Mama had many exceptional abilities, most of which do not appear in this story. She could face down a T Rex. Humans were more difficult for her. They made her uneasy and put her off her game.

way to tell the species. Since this was Earth, the logical first guess was a human, which meant humans had discovered how to make a working time machine. This by itself was not a huge problem, but the humans in question were clearly using the machine irresponsibly; and they were using it irresponsibly in an era she considered her own. She had to nip this in the bud.

She took off along the trail left by the hunter. At first it was easy to follow. Soon it led onto harder ground. The vegetation changed to conifers, with ferns growing in open spaces. Sometimes she made out a scuff mark in the fallen needles or saw a crushed fern. But it was slow work. She had to stop often, bend over, and peer. Small things distracted her: a delicate flower, blooming amid the ferns; the flash of a small mammal running like hell away from her; a pile of manure left by a not-especially-large dinosaur. Even though she had a mission, she was a woman in love with sensation.

"What the hell are you doing here?" a voice asked as she gazed at the poop.

She straightened up and turned. There stood a human dressed in hunter's camouflage. His pants were blood stained, and he held a rifle. He looked Big Red Mama up and down, then grinned. It wasn't a nice grin. At this point, she remembered that she was wearing no clothes.

Why should she? The local bugs had not yet evolved to prey on large mammals, and she knew which plants to avoid. Clothing chaffed and got in the way. She liked the feeling of wind against her skin, the heat of sunlight, the cool touch of rain.

"Not that I'm complaining," said the hunter. "You *are* a looker, though I've never seen skin of that particular intense shade of red. Are you Native American?"

"I am native wherever I am," said Big Red Mama, "and that includes here and now. What are you doing in my geologic era?"

"*Your* geologic era?" the man said. "You have a lot of guts. In case you haven't noticed, this is a long time before property laws. I suppose that might change, if time travel catches on. People will show up and stake claims and subdivide." He gave her another nasty grin. "Time-share condos in the age of dinosaurs! You can bet they will sell! I might want to get in on the ground floor."

"Did you invent time travel?" asked Big Red Mama.

"My brother did. He's an eccentric genius and inventor—and too dumb to realize what I was going to do, when he told me that he had a way to travel through time."

"What was that?" asked Big Red Mama. There were several ways to take care of this situation, including one that had just appeared behind the man, moving quietly. Amazing that something of Albert's size could step with so much care! In the meantime, before she decided what exactly to do, she wanted to find out about the time machine.

The man grinned. "I hit him over the head and locked him in a closet. That seemed like a good short-term solution. I might need him again. What if there's something about the machine that I don't know and can't figure out? Though I asked him to show me everything, and I think he did. What a fool!"

"Why are you telling me this?"

"Why not? There's no one here you can tell."

"Are you sure?" asked Big Red Mama.

Albert had stopped and was standing behind the man, as motionless as a heron waiting for fish. His head was cocked. One bright eye watched her. His open mouth revealed teeth like knives.

The man frowned. "Are you telling me there are other people here?"

There weren't, and Big Red Mama didn't like to lie. She answered by saying, "How do you think I got here? Don't you imagine other people might be able to use the same mode of transport?"

Her relatives, the other Big Mamas and Poppas, could time travel the same way she did, using force of character rather than a machine. But none was in the Cretaceous at the moment. She knew that for certain. They all had good manners and would have stopped by to say hello.

"I was thinking of keeping you around, at least till I'm ready to leave," the man said. "But if there are other people here…"

He'd been holding his rifle across his chest, the muzzle pointing to the side and up. This showed that he had been trained in gun safety. Big Red Mama approved. But now his arms and shoulders tensed—just a little, but enough to tell her that he was about to change the rifle's position. Most likely he would point it at her and pull the trigger. It was clearly time to act. Big Red Mama moved her hand, signaling Albert.

"What?" said the man and began to turn. He was half way around, when he saw what bounded toward him. "My god!" he shouted and pulled the trigger without pausing to aim. The bullet sped into the cloudless blue sky, and Albert reached the man. His long teeth closed on the rifle barrel. His head jerked up, whipping the rifle out of the hunter's hands. Albert took a step back and cocked an eye at his mistress.

"Good boy," said Big Red Mama. "And you," she added to the man, "keep perfectly still. Albert is very well trained; but he is a predator, and he does have hunting instincts. If you start to struggle, he's likely to give in to them."

"My god," the man repeated, not moving.

"His name is Albert," she added. "But he isn't an Albertosaurus. I suppose I could have named him Al or Ally, but I've never liked those names, and even when he was a hatchling, he looked like an Albert. He's a dwarf Allosaurus, not native to this region. He belongs in the far south, in a region that will become part of Australia but is now part of Antarctica. Think of him as a creature of the midnight sun, the southern aurora, and a climate cold enough so he needs feathers. Aren't they lovely?"

His back was dark, iridescent green, his belly pale green. His throat shone like a hummingbird's. She couldn't imagine a lovelier therapod.

"I raised him from the egg," she added proudly. "You'd be surprised how intelligent he is. You must never think lizard, when you think of dinosaurs. Think bird. The best of them—the hunters especially—are as bright as a parrot or maybe brighter. I have never trained a parrot."

She walked over and took the rifle, then moved to a safe distance and leveled the gun at the man. "I could talk all day about Albert, but we need to talk about you."

"You have to let me go back," the man said quickly. "If I stay here, it'll cause a paradox. My brother said any little thing can change history. You step on a butterfly in the age of the dinosaurs, and the Nazis win the Second World War or the Red Sox win the world series."

"You didn't think about that when you killed that dinosaur or when you thought about killing me," said Big Red

Mama, ignoring the reference to the Nazis and Red Socks. She remembered the Nazis: a nasty lot, worse than small-town Americans in the nineteenth century.[2] Were the Red Socks similar? Red socks and brown shirts? Not a combination she would wear.

"I wasn't going to kill you," the man said.

"Yes, you were, sooner or later, most likely after raping me. I have never been raped," Big Red Mama said. "And as much as I like experiences of many kinds, that is one I don't intend to have."

The man looked uneasy. "There's a time and place for everything, and everything has to be in its place and time. That's what my brother told me. All you can do is observe. There's no safe way to take anything back to the present, except information. And what good is information from the past? If I could go into the future, that would be different; but my brother says it's impossible to travel into the future. It doesn't exist yet."

The hunter's brother had a lot of bad information. For the most part, time was self-healing. Trying to change it was like trying to kick a hole in a river. The hole closed; the river flowed on; and everything was the same downstream. If you had the resources, you could make a real change to the past, just as you could make a real change to the present. But it required considerable resources. Something like the U.S. Army Corps of Engineers could do the job, though the result you got might not be one you expected or liked. Tame the Mississippi, turn it into a shipping canal, and lose the port at the end of the canal, if not at once, then over time.

....

2 Remembering the future is a neat trick, but not difficult, once you have time travel.

As for the future, it existed as much as the past or present. It had to exist for time travel to be possible. Once one can travel through time at different speeds and in more than one direction, then all time becomes relative; and every point in time (except the first) is sometimes in the future and sometimes in the past. The Cretaceous was the Permian's future. The hunter's home, whenever it might be, was her future, at least at the moment. She might decide to take a journey to the twenty-fifth century, when humans whizzed among the stars and spoke a language that was a distant descendant of this man's English. When she did that, this man's home would be in her past.

Big Purple Poppa, who loved math, said the equations for time travel were elegant as all heck. But she was not especially good at math; and when she tried to describe time travel using words, she got a really terrible headache. It was better just to do it and not think too much.

None of this mattered at the moment. The man had a time machine, and if the technology got around, she would be dealing with vacation homes in the Cretaceous. They weren't likely to change history, since the dinosaurs were doomed anyway. But they could make her life a pain.

"Take me to your machine," she said.

The man looked hesitant.

"I don't think history requires you, here or anywhen else," she added. "If I shoot you or have Albert tear you apart, nothing will change, except for you."

"That isn't what my brother said."

"Your brother's opinion doesn't matter. My opinion matters, and I think I can shoot you in perfect safety."

The man shuddered and led her up a slope. Albert followed, his head tilted so he could watch the man. At the top of the slope was a meadow full of ferns.

"Shit," the man said.

"What?" she asked.

"It should be here."

They walked to the center of the meadow. There was a rectangular area where the ferns had been crushed.

The man pointed. "I left it here."

"Where are you from?" Big Red Mama asked.

The man hesitated again. She moved her hand, and Albert hissed loudly.

"December 15, 2013," the man said.

"What address?"

"211 Prairie Drive, Morris, Minnesota. It's my brother's home and lab."

Big Red Mama nodded and made a gesture to Albert. "He's going to guard you. If you try to leave this meadow, he'll rip your guts out and eat them. Stay put! I'll be back."

Using force of character, she moved to a new time and place.

An icy wind swept past her. She was knee-deep in snow. Flakes whirled under street lamps. In front of her, warm light shone through the windows of a large, low house. She waded to the front door and rang the bell. After a moment, the door opened. A tall, lanky man stood in the doorway, outlined by yellow light. There was an ugly bruise on his forehead; one side of his face was swollen, and his glasses had been repaired with electrical tape. He was going to have one heck of a shiner, Big Red Mama thought.

"You're naked," he said to her.

"That isn't important."

"In this weather it is. You're going to freeze! Come in, unless— Is there any chance that you're crazy? Why are you carrying a rifle?"

"I took it away from your brother."

"Brad? Good for you. Come in, before you get frostbite."

She entered. The hall led to a good-sized living room. The floor was tile, dotted with Navaho rugs. The walls were pine. A fire burned in a big, stone fireplace. A very pleasant place, Big Red Mama thought.

"I'll get you something to wear," the man said and left.

She stood in front of the fire, dripping melting snow. The man came back with a terry cloth bathrobe. "Put this on; and please put down the rifle. It makes me nervous."

She laid it across a table and put on the robe. There was something likable about the man. He reminded her of Albert: dangerous and anxious to please. Anyone who could build a time machine was dangerous. In addition, she saw a gleam of danger in his keen blue eyes.

"Can I get you anything? Coffee? Hot chocolate? A glass of wine?"

"Wine," said Big Red Mama, feeling a little shy, as she always did around good-looking, dangerous men with manners.

He came back with a full glass. "It's a country red from Minnesota, where the grapes can suffer and learn from their suffering."

"What?"

"It's a local joke and out of date. It barely snows in the Twin Cities these days, which is one reason I don't live there; and every time it snows out here, I think—this may be the last real storm. Maybe, after this, there will be nothing but flurries and freezing rain." He grinned, an angry baring of teeth that reminded her of his brother. "Wintry mix, the weather bureau calls it. I call it crap. I want the storms we had when I was kid. Where is Brad?"

She sipped the wine. It was harsh, but comforting—like reality, she thought. Maybe it did grapes good to suffer. "He's in the late Cretaceous, being guarded by a dwarf Allosaurus."

"No kidding! He's not hurt, is he?"

"Why do you care?"

The man touched the bruise on his forehead and winced. "He's my brother. I have to care. I'm Thaddeus Peterson. Everyone calls me Pete." He held his hand out, and she shook it. But she had no name to give him.

"You built the time machine," she said.

"Yeah." He smiled shyly. "It worked, didn't it? I figured Brad would want to try it out. Though I didn't figure he would hit me and stuff me in a closet." Pete shrugged. "No problem. The house is smart. As soon as I came to, I told it to let me out.

"Brad has always been a problem, but he has more physical courage than I do. I figured he would be the perfect person to test the machine."

"He went back to the Cretaceous and killed a dinosaur. I think he would have killed me or raped me or done both, if he'd been able."

Pete frowned and winced again. "I tried to make sure he wouldn't do any harm. I told him the future didn't exist, so there was no point in trying to go there; and I told him he must not do anything in the past, because it might change history. I guess he didn't believe me—or didn't care."

She thought of asking him if he really believed what he'd told his brother, but decided not to. Time might be as difficult to change as a wide river rolling majestically toward whatever (if anything) existed at the end of time. But it was possible to change and harm the lives of beings who lived in various eras. Imagine a river town attacked by pirates or bandits. What happened would not change the river, but it would certainly change the lives of the people in the town.

As a group, humans underestimated the damage they did and rarely took responsibility for anything. It was never a good idea to give them anything they could use as an excuse. Let Pete think that time was easy to change. It was better than thinking there were no consequences.

She asked him how he discovered time travel.

"By accident."

This made sense to Big Red Mama. Almost everyone who discovered time travel did so by accident, since it appeared to violate a basic law of physics: effect must follow cause, and you can't kill your own grandfather.[3]

Pete waved at a pair of comfortable-looking chairs in front of the fire. "Please sit down."

Big Red Mama settled in one, the man in the other. She stretched out her long, sleek, red legs and wiggled her bare, red toes. The man looked appreciative.

"I own a company that does computer design. The company headquarters are in the Twin Cities and so are the company labs. But my personal lab is here in Morris, west of the house, with nothing between it and the Rockies except prairie and wind. I grew up in Morris. So did Brad. Our dad was a professor at the U of M campus here. Brad left as soon as he could, but I came back after I finished my postdoc work. I like it." He glanced around at the comfort-

....
3 Well, yes and no. This will be discussed later.

able living room, firelight dancing on the black tile floor. "This, and the prairie, and the wind, and the U. There's no place I'd rather be. I guess you could call me a real Midwesterner."

Not her favorite kind of person, thought Big Red Mama. But this man seemed pleasant. She wiggled her toes again, and the man noticed with evident pleasure.

"I'm trying to figure out what I can tell you. A lot of it is proprietary information."

"What does that mean?" Big Red Mama asked.

"It means I own it, but the patents have not yet been filed."

Aha, thought Big Red Mama. She had arrived at the right moment. In general, she believed that information wants to be free; but in this case, she was willing to make an exception.

"We've been working on a new chip. " He paused. "I think it's safe to tell you it's a quantum chip. Plenty of people are working on those these days. But we knew we were ahead of everyone else.

"We got a chip that worked. I can tell you that much; and I can say the chip was erratic. Sometimes it worked perfectly. We put information in, and — zap! — information came out, and it was exactly the information we wanted and expected. Other times, the right information came out, but there was a delay of minutes or hours or even days. Sometimes we got nothing; and sometimes information came out when we had put nothing in. That was really interesting, and so were the times when the chip gave us the answer to a question we were thinking about asking.

"Whatever it was doing would not help our customers, who wanted fast, reliable answers to real-world questions;

and it wasn't something I wanted to take to investors. Not yet. Not until I understood the chip.

"I told the guys at the company labs to move on to other problems, and I took the chip home to Morris. I guess you could call me a loner. I certainly wanted to work on the chip alone.

"I built a computer using the chip, just to see what would happen." He grinned. "I kept losing the operating system. It would be there, then gone, then back. The same thing happened to the applications. The files were hell. I never knew what was going to be in them. A lot of the time, I couldn't read them.

"I kept tinkering, and then I started losing the entire machine. It would be there, then gone, then back. Sometimes when it came back it had modifications that hadn't been present when it vanished. Some of them were really useful. I realized I had something interesting, though I wasn't sure what. At first I thought it might be teleportation, though that wouldn't explain the changes that happened to the machine...

"Now I think it was fluctuating around the present. Sometimes it would go into the near future and come back with changes I had made. Sometimes it would go into the recent past and lose the changes. I'm not a theoretician. I don't know what the underlying physics is. Quantum uncertainty?"

He set his glass on the floor, got up, and went to the fireplace. There were animal figures on the mantel, made of red stone and inlaid with turquoise, onyx, and coral. One was a bear like a Zuni fetish. Another was a stylized bison. The third was a turtle.

Big Red Mama had a lot of odd bits of information and an interest in Native American culture. She knew these were Indian work from the late twentieth or early twenty-first century, done in the last days of white rule in North America, before the Great Midwestern Earthquake brought an empire down, and little red people flooded into the ruins from the south. Soon, North American Indian artists would be borrowing from their Aztec and Mayan cousins, and Day of the Dead skeletons would be dancing across the Midwest.

Pete fiddled with the figures. "I could have gone to my investors then, or to the Department of Defense. But I wanted to understand what was going on. So I kept going, until I got…" He stopped for a moment. "You must know all of this, if you come from the Cretaceous. You couldn't have been there, unless you have your own time machine."

Big Red Mama was silent, not liking to lie.

Pete turned, looking suddenly wary. "Did you come from the past? Did Brad go there? I didn't see him go. Maybe he loaded the machine into a truck and drove it off. Maybe you come from him.

"Or maybe you're an industrial spy. I've had them sniffing around me before. Or a real spy, from some place like China or the European Union."[4]

Enough of this, Big Red Mama thought. She stood up and moved to the Permian, to a rocky shore just before the catastrophe that ended Permian life. The tide was out. In the debris at the high water mark, she found a small trilobite. She carried it back to Pete in Morris,

....

4 Why hadn't he thought of this before? Big Red Mama exerts a powerful influence, especially when she's naked.

Minnesota, at the start of the twenty-first century and put it in his hand.

"My god," he said, staring at the little creature as it crawled the length of his open palm and tumbled onto the floor. He bent quickly and picked it up.

"Three-lobed shell," said Big Red Mama. "Large compound eyes. Many little legs. Do you recognize it?"

"It's a living trilobite," said Pete. "You just sort of flickered, and then you were gone, and then you were back, and then you handed me a living trilobite."

"Yes," she said. "I got it from the end of the Permian, and I don't want to hear any more crap about spying."

"Where is your machine? You can't have hidden it about your person, not when you arrived without clothes."

"We aren't talking about my machine," Big Red Mama said. "We're talking about yours."

"Either it's small and embedded in your body, or it operates at a distance," Pete said, looking intrigued.

"I said we're talking about your machine," Big Red Mama repeated.

He was holding the trilobite between thumb and forefinger. The tiny legs scrabbled, trying to get traction. "I know a guy at the university who would love to see this fellow."

"Your machine," said Big Red Mama firmly.

"I'm not going to tell you anything more about it," he replied with equal firmness. "If you have a machine, you know the rest of the story. If you don't, I have not a clue where you got this critter."

"And you are the only person who knows about the machine?" Big Red Mama asked.

Pete looked more wary than before.

She grabbed his arm and yanked him into the Cretaceous. They arrived in the fern meadow. Brad was there, along with Albert.

"My god," said Pete, staring at the Allosaurus.

"Where's the time machine, jerk?" asked Brad.

"Back home in Morris, I expect," said Pete. "It has a timer and a homing device. How do you think I got it back, when I was testing it?"

"You were willing to maroon me here?" Brad asked with indignation.

"I would have told you about the homing device, if you'd given me time. But you hit me on the head and shoved me in a closet. You have always been a loser, Brad, ever since you ran away when you were seventeen."

"And you — the good boy — stayed at home and went to MIT," Brad replied. "Just the way our jerk father wanted."

The two men were face to face. Twins, Big Red Mama realized. More than that, they were identical twins. Strange. She had always thought that identical twins got along.[5]

"Yes," said Pete with satisfaction. "And got a good education and made a fortune. More than you can say."

"I've traveled all over the world, you jerk, and screwed more women and had more fun than you can possibly imagine. What the hell good has your money done you? You sit in your lab in Morris and do nothing, except your damn science. You could do anything, anything!"

....

5 Why hadn't Big Red Mama noticed the resemblance between the brothers earlier? (a) She had not seen the two men together before this. (b) She might have been misled by the whacking great bruise on Pete's forehead, his swollen face, and his damaged glasses. (c) Their resemblance might be increasing.

The loud voices were making Albert nervous. He honked like a large goose. Both men glanced at him briefly, then went back to glaring at each other. Fools, thought Big Red Mama. One does not ignore a good-sized dinosaur.

But the brothers were busy with each other. As they glared, silent for the moment, their edges began to flicker and spread sideways, until they formed two rows of men, extending to the edge of the fern meadow and maybe farther. If so, the shadows of the forest hid them. The rows faced each other, glaring.

Pete — all the Petes — stepped forward and put a hand on all the Brads. Was there going to be a fight? Big Red Mama wondered. No. Instead, there was another flicker, a big one.

The two rows merged, becoming a single row of men, all identical, except that they were facing alternating directions. First there was a Brad — or Pete — facing east, then a Pete — or Brad — facing west, then another Brad and another Pete, one looking east, the other looking west, then another and another, back and forth, over and over, to the edges of the forest.

Albert honked again, this time sounding seriously worried. The feathers on his jaws lifted, forming an iridescent ruff. The men turned, so all of them were facing Albert. They looked at the Allosaurus with identical wary expressions. This was smart. The raised ruff was a challenge. Albert was getting ready to confront.

Then, while Big Red Mama watched with continuing surprise, the row of men contracted, collapsing into a single man.

For a moment, the man stood upright and alone. Then he collapsed onto the ground.

Albert honked a third time. This time the noise was plaintive, as if the dinosaur were asking, *what the heck?*

"I know how you feel," Big Red Mama said and walked to the fallen man. She knelt and felt his throat. The pulse was strong and steady. He had merely fainted.

"Guard him," she told Albert and went back to Morris. The rifle was still in the house. She picked it up. Out back was a long, low building, much larger than the house. The lab. Its door was locked. Standing knee-deep in snow, she peered in through a window and saw a platform in the middle of a large, bare room. Bright lights shone down on it. At the platform's center was a plastic and metal contraption about the size of an old-fashioned phone booth. Small bits of greenery clung to its lower edges: pieces of fern, still unwilted, though they were 65 million years old.

There would be time to deal with the machine later. First she had to deal with the man.

A moment later, she was back in the Cretaceous. The man was sitting up in the middle of the mashed area where the time machine had been. His face was pale. There was no bruise on his forehead. Did this mean he was Brad? He was wearing glasses, like Pete, but they no longer had—or needed—an electrical tape repair.

"Who are you?" she asked.

"Thaddeus Bradley Peterson," he replied.

What did that mean? she wondered. Had the two brothers merged? She asked the question out loud.

"I have no brother," the man replied. "I am an only child."

Albert honked sadly, possibly remembering the clutch of eggs from which he and his brothers and sisters hatched. Most likely, not.

The man stood shakily. "I wanted a brother, especially after my mother died. It was so hard living with my father! He wanted so much for me and from me! I was supposed to be a genius and a good boy." He took off his glasses and rubbed his face. "The strange thing is, I gave him what he wanted. I am a genius; and I have always been a very good boy, even after I grew up and Dad retired and moved to Florida.

"I didn't want to be. I wanted to run away and have adventures and pay no attention — none at all! — to what other people wanted." He frowned. "The time machine worked fine in trials. Almost all the mice came back. I thought I could try it myself. But something happened. You can't believe how strange my memories are. I feel as if I've been two people."

This was interesting and unexpected, Big Red Mama thought. When the man went back into the past, he became another self, leaving the first self in Morris in the twenty-first century. This had never happened to her or her relatives. Maybe this kind of trans-temporal bifurcation required a time machine; or maybe the Big Mamas and Poppas were so entirely themselves that they could not chose alternate ways to be.[6]

"You have been two people," she told the man. "And one of you has been a jerk. Are you a jerk now?"

The man frowned. "I don't think so. Though I don't feel as smart or conscientious as I used to feel. I would like to have sex with a beautiful woman. I would like to have an adventure, maybe one that is risqué."

....

6 The story of Big Green Mama on the planet of the Skwork suggests otherwise, but Big Red Mama did not know this story at this time.

"That can be arranged," said Big Red Mama. "But first we have to torch your lab."

"Why?"

"I don't want humans to learn about time travel; though if you—as an individual—want to visit the twenty-second century, that can be arranged. You really don't want to live through the twenty-first century. It's going to be a nightmare."

The man considered for a long moment, then nodded. Big Red Mama grabbed his hand and took him to Morris at the start of the twenty-first century. There was firewood stacked by the house and gasoline in the pearl-white Cadillac pickup truck inside Pete's four-car garage. Working quickly, they built a fire and lit it. Once the lab was burning well, she led him into the future.

Did she make love to him there?

No, but he found many beautiful women, some of them genetically female and human, and elevators that rose into space; and space ships that visited all the planets in the solar system; and animals that had been engineered to look like dinosaurs and mammoths and trilobites. There were no time machines. He didn't miss them. Instead, he enjoyed being a new person—not a genius and not entirely good, but good enough to get by in the future, where there was enough wealth to provide for every single person and anyone could go to the stars. Sometimes the flow of history leads to a major disaster, like the end of the Cretaceous or the Permian. Sometimes it leads to a minor disaster, like the twenty-first century; and sometimes it leads to marvels and delights.

After she left Pete in the twenty-second century, Big Red Mama stopped in Morris to retrieve the trilobite and return it to its home. She did not do this to avoid a paradox, but because there was a limit to how long trilobites can survive out of water. It would not have been kind to leave the poor little creature to die on a living room floor 251 million years after its native era. She put it down tenderly on the Permian sand and watched it crawl into the Permian ocean, then returned to her current home in the Cretaceous.

Albert still looked ruffled and worried. She soothed him down, and they went for a walk through the Cretaceous forest. Both of them enjoyed the scent of conifers and ferns and early flowering trees. Some of the flowers were pollinated by bees and smelled sweet, like honey. Others were pollinated by carrion flies and smelled liked rotten meat. Big Red Mama enjoyed even these last. She was a woman in love with sensation, and though the odor was a bit difficult, the flowers themselves—bright red like fresh blood or like her—were lovely.

A while later, Big Purple Poppa came by for a visit. He was not a close relative, but he was one of her favorites: a huge, royal purple fellow with a splendid physique. Like most of the Mamas and Poppas, he wasn't much for clothing. However, he wore a strap diagonally across his chest so he had a place to attach his nerd pack, which was full of double zero drafting pens. Big Purple Poppa liked a fine point. He also wore glasses with thick, black frames. He didn't need the glasses, but he thought they made him look more intelligent.

She told him about Pete and Brad.

He nodded, looking thoughtful. "Strange things happen when you connect the macro world with the quantum level of reality. Fortunately, due to emergence, different rules apply at the macro level, and the quantum weirdness is usually only transitory." He broke off a horsetail growing nearby and used it to draw a diagram in the damp beach sand, showing what happens when you go back in time and kill your grandfather:

You discover that you are five inches shorter, because your grandmother married the nice Chinese man next door, after the mysterious death of her first husband; and he is your grandfather, not the guy you just killed for reasons you will never understand. All along the chain of cause and effect that leads to this moment, small adjustments happen, until this event — you standing with a dead man at your feet — becomes possible and even likely. You are tried for murder and executed, never knowing exactly what happened and why you did what you did. This is too bad, but it explains many mysterious crimes.

You vanish, having never existed, since your grandmother never remarried and had no children. Your grandfather is now alive, though with a slight headache. He produces children and grandchildren, and one of the latter is you. You go back in time and kill him. You vanish.

He is alive again. You kill him again. This continues until you get tired of it.

"You can think of the first as a slight eddy in the river of time," said Big Poppa. "And the second is a whirlpool. In either case, the river keeps going, being a sum of all the ripples and eddies and whirlpools in it.

"Effect does follow cause, but causal lines do not always move in the same direction as time. It is possible to swim upstream like a salmon and die before you are born, though salmon don't—in fact—usually do this. You should never confuse your own life with time in general or the history of the universe. Hegel was wrong."

"Who?" asked Big Red Mama.

"Georg Wilhelm Friedrich Hegel, a German philosopher who overestimated the influence of individuals on history."

"Oh," said Big Red Mama.

"All of this makes sense to me," Big Purple Poppa added. "But I don't know why Pete became two people. It must have something to do with quantum uncertainty, but I don't know what."

Big Red Mama didn't care. She was enjoying the moment. Albert had wandered off, possibly looking for a mate, though he would find none in this era. She was standing with a handsome, royal purple man on a lovely beach, while pterosaurs glided in the distance, looking for fish.

The Cretaceous would end, but not yet. Its doom still drifted in the Oort Belt. Most likely it had not yet begun its long trip in from the outer darkness. In the meantime, she would feel the ocean wind flipping her hair and smell the salt water and admire Big Purple Poppa.[7]

....

7 Time travel was discovered again of course, as an accidental result of the Lunar Very, Very Large Collider, which began operation at the end of the twenty-second century. Shortly thereafter, the time police were created to do traffic control and make sure the eras before time travel were mostly left alone. Big Red Mama and her relatives ran into the time police now and then. They greeted each other with respect, though they traveled in different ways and had different ideas of time. Still, they were not a threat to one another, and there is room in the universe for many ideas and many modes of travel.

BIG BROWN MAMA AND BRER RABBIT

Big Brown Mama could be any shade she wanted, from a *café au lait* so pale it seemed the *café* had barely walked past the *lait*, right down to a dark, rich mahogany. She could have been black, too, but she avoided that hue out of respect for Big Black Mama. Big Black had claimed her color back when human beings were just starting to be human. The Big Mamas and Poppas had just come into existence then and were sorting themselves out, deciding how they wanted to look and what they wanted to be. All they knew for certain was, they wanted to be individual. Big Black Mama picked black, and Big Brown Mama picked brown. Other Big Mamas and Poppas looked around and picked leaf-green, sky-blue, lion-yellow, termite-white, red-dirt-red, till they had claimed all the colors of Africa. Later on, they claimed all the colors of Earth and the galaxy and the great, wide universe.

How could they claim so much? They had a lot of ability. They could walk across a galaxy as if it were a city park, and up and down the arrow of time as if it were a two-way street. Nothing scared them. If a black hole tried to swallow them, they'd reach in past its event horizon, grab hold of the singularity in its center, give a good jerk, and pull it inside out, so it became a white hole, spewing matter from who knew where.

They kept away from the big holes at galactic centers. Everyone should know his or her limits; and they didn't want to wreck a galaxy.

But that isn't what this story is about.

Imagine Big Brown Mama on a summer day in Minneapolis at the start of the twenty-first century. She was a big woman, broad and solid, with plenty of curves and the face of an Ife queen. She didn't have the scarification of an Ife queen, since that would have looked out of place in the middle of the United States. Instead, her face was smooth and creamy brown, with really fine makeup. Like all the Mamas, she was a good dresser when she chose to be. On this occasion she wore a pure white linen suit with a skirt that stopped well above the knee. It was completely unwrinkled, though this is contrary to nature, which says that linen will wrinkle if you look at it. Her shoes were sling-backed high heels, and as high as they were, she had no trouble walking. Her hair was twisted into little dreadlocks. Large, glittering earrings hung from her ears. If you could have looked closely, you would have seen they were spiral galaxies. Now and then, one flashed. People thought the earring was reflecting light. Not a bit. It was a supernova exploding. The earrings were real galaxies, though a bit on the small side, and Big Brown Mama liked her galaxies lively.

Click, click she went on her impossibly high heels, walking down the Nicollet Mall in downtown Minneapolis. It was early evening, a little after six. The sun was still high in the sky, and the air was more than warm. Now and then, someone thought of saying, "Yo, Mama," or "Hey, babe!"

She looked at them before they spoke, and the words shriveled in their mouths. Their tongues curled. Their male apparatuses retreated into their bodies. They considered whether they might want to take up a life of religion or go on a long journey, perhaps to Antarctica. Big Brown Mama believed in respect.

"Pardon me," a man said courteously.

She glanced over. He was big and black, maybe fifty years old, wearing blue jeans and a yellow tee-shirt that said, "Lac Courte Oreilles Band of Ojibwe." His short hair was graying. He looked bone tired, and he had big, long, floppy rabbit ears.

This startled her. "You a rabbit," she said, her tone between a comment and a question.

The man looked surprised. "You know that?"

"I know what I see," said Big Brown Mama. "And what I see is a rabbit."

"There's a bar here," the man said. "Do you want to go in and talk?"

Of course she did. She was nothing if not curious, and a woman who wore galaxies for earrings could not object to a man with big, floppy ears.

They entered the cool darkness. A polite white person seated them. The bar was a jazz club. According to a sign, the music would begin in two hours.

"How'd you know I'm a rabbit?" the man asked.

"I can see your ears."

He looked surprised a second time. "Most people can't."

"I am not most people."

A white waitress arrived. They ordered drinks: a whiskey for him, straight up with ice water on the side, and a chardonnay for her. She was a chardonnay sort of woman and spent most of her time in eras and on planets where it was easily available.

The drinks came. He took a deep swallow of water, then a sip of whiskey. "Now that is *good*."

Big Brown Mama sipped her own drink and eyed him. No question he was a rabbit, though not an ordinary one. Somehow he had gotten inside a human body, which he wore like a tired, old, threadbare suit. He'd been in there for a long, long time.

"How'd you get in there?" she asked the rabbit.

"It's a story and not a short one," he answered in his deep man's voice.

"I like stories," Big Brown Mama said firmly. "You tell it, and I'll listen; and if that nice young white woman comes around a second time, I think I'll have a Cobb salad with blue cheese dressing and some dinner rolls and maybe some dessert later on."

The rabbit man laughed a deep, rich laugh. "Yes, ma'am."

"I like a man with respect."

The waitress came back, and they ordered dinner. The man had a BLT.

"It's too hot for meat, and I'm mostly a vegetarian."

When the nice young white woman left them, he began his story. He told it like a made-up, fictional story, maybe because it was too strange to believe, or maybe because Big Brown Mama had a powerful influence on her environment, and she did like a well-told story, no matter how fantastic.

How Brer Rabbit Got To Detroit

One day Brer Rabbit left his home in the pine woods and went romping through the cotton fields, looking for trouble. There was nothing he liked better than causing a ruckus. It was spring, and the cotton plants were budding; and there—on the top of a cotton bud—sat a little bug with a long snout, like nothing he had ever seen before.

Brer Rabbit stopped. "What are you?"

"I'm a boll weevil. I came from Texas looking for a new home, and this is going to be it." The bug looked around. "Mighty fine eating here. I'm going to send word back to Texas for everyone to come."

Well, Brer Rabbit didn't pay a lot of attention. What kind of trouble could a little bug cause? So he went hopping along, enjoying the spring day, thinking how fine life was. It was for him, but all around him were people working hard and barely getting by. Brer Rabbit didn't care, not then.

He was right that one boll weevil was not much of a problem. But it must have sent word back to Texas. Either that, or it was mighty prolific. Soon enough, he'd be lolloping through the cotton fields, and there'd be weevils everywhere, sticking their long snouts into the cotton buds and sucking the life out of them. When they weren't eating, they'd be singing in high voices that were barely audible:

> Boll weevil's here, boll weevil's everywhere.
> Boll weevil's gonna rob you of your home.

It was a mean song, and Brer Rabbit didn't like it. But what could he do? He talked to Brer Bear and Brer Fox and Old Man Terrapin. None of them could see a way to get rid of the weevils.

"Maybe it won't matter to us," Brer Fox said. "We live in the pine woods, and those weevils don't eat pines."

Old Man Terrapin shook his scaly head. "These are bad times, and I don't see them getting better."

Brer Bear was silent a long time. At last he said, "All I know is, I can't eat those bugs without getting a mouthful of cotton. There's better bugs in a honey bee hive or a rotten log."

Even worse than their sucking and singing, the weevils laid eggs. Their children were nasty-looking maggots that chewed into the cotton bolls and ate them from the inside out. The bolls died and fell off into the red dirt or rotted on the stem. Entire fields were dying, rotting in the summer sun.

Now Brer Rabbit could see that the weevils' song was true. Without a cash crop, farmers couldn't pay the rent on their land. If times did not get better, people were going to lose their homes.

At first people hoped the weevils would leave. Instead, more and more kept coming. Like the song said:

> The first time I saw the weevil, he was sitting on
> a square.
> The next time I saw him, he had his family there.

A square was a cotton bud, though it was like a town square to the weevils, standing in crowds, their long snouts in the air, like hound dogs finding a scent. They were smell-ing food and ruin.

It was no longer possible to bring in a harvest, though people kept trying for a while. They got nothing for their work except fields of rotting, maggot-infested cotton bolls.

Finally people realized that nothing was going to get better. The weevils were staying, and there was no way to raise cotton with them around.

They sat on their front porches and talked about what to do next. Some folks wanted to go to the Mississippi Delta. River flooding drowned the weevils there, so they couldn't stay alive from year to year; and it was still pos-sible to grow cotton. Other folks said it'd be better to take their chances up north. No Jim Crow up there. A man could vote. There were jobs in the factories.

Brer Rabbit crouched in the darkness, as close as he could get without being seen. What would it be like if the people left? No gardens for him. No hens for Brer Fox. No music on the porches in the evening, and no dances by lantern light. Life would be a lot less interesting and tasty.

After that, people began packing. Some went west to the delta. Others started north. Sometimes the men went alone. Sometimes families went, starting out in wagons or on foot, everything they owned on their backs or in their hands.

Behind them, the landlords went through their papers and added up their numbers and wondered how they were going to survive, with farmhouses empty and the fields full of rotting cotton.

"We'll be fine," Brer Fox said in a worried tone. "I don't need chickens. I just like them."

"Good riddance," said Brer Coon. "They won't be hunting raccoons now, or if they do, it won't be me and my family."

Brer Rabbit wasn't sure of this. Used to be, the cotton kept everyone busy. It was a hard crop that never stopped needing work. Without it, the folks who remained would have more time for hunting and fishing, and they'd be hungry, without money to buy store food. If they had gardens, they'd guard them closely.

It didn't seem to him that life was going to be easier. He knew he'd miss all those gardens full of fresh vegetables, and he'd miss the music. He couldn't tell what he liked more: the singing at night on front porches, or the singing in churches on Sunday morning, before the day got hot. He'd be lolloping along in the morning shadows of the pine woods, and that music would come to him across the cool morning air. Sweet! Like the taste of new lettuce or a spring onion!

He thought and thought about it. In the end, he decided to go north. But he couldn't go as a rabbit. He was pretty sure of that. From what he heard, it was a long way. Too far to hop, which meant he'd have to find some other way to travel. People weren't too likely to offer a ride to a rabbit, unless they decided that he could be dinner. If he was going to make it north safely, he needed to be a man.

So he waited till it rained, and then he dug up some wet, red dirt and shaped it into a man. Looked pretty natural lying on the ground, Brer Rabbit thought. If he could just get inside and wear the clay body like a coat, he'd be fine. The problem was, how was he going to get inside? He thought a while, then took a jump, landing — splat! — in the middle of the clay man's chest. Clay went flying, and there he sat in the hole his jump had made. Clots of clay hung in his fur; and there were lumps of clay all around him, none of them looking like a man or anything else.

He climbed out of the hole and tried to brush the clay out of his fur.

That hadn't worked. But Brer Rabbit could be stubborn, so stubborn that he made himself a fool. He wasn't ready to give up. So he got more clay and tried again. Around the third or fourth try, Ma Johnson came by. She was an old woman, thin as a stick and as black as tar, with sharp eyes and a nose like a hatchet. Part Indian, folks said. That's where she got her magic.

"What you doing?" she asked Brer Rabbit. Most people couldn't talk to animals, but she could.

"I'm trying to make a man and get inside him," Brer Rabbit replied.

"Why?"

Brer Rabbit explained that he wanted to go north.

"So do I," said Ma Johnson. "I hear good things about Detroit. Mr. Henry Ford is hiring black folks and paying good wages. There's gonna be black people up there with money, who might need the services I provide.

"But I don't want to go alone. I could use a big, strong man to help me along the way. If I get you into that body, will you promise to travel with me?"

Brer Rabbit thought for a moment, then nodded. It might be foolish, but he really did want to go. The empty houses and the fields of dying cotton were getting on his nerves.

He never figured out what happened next. One moment, he was nodding his agreement with Ma Johnson's proposal. Then there was an empty space in his memory, like he'd had a fit or a deep sleep with no dreams. When he woke, he was in the clay body, and it was climbing up onto its feet. It was night, though it hadn't been before; and a round, fat, yellow moon shone down on him.

Ma Johnson was in front of him, leaning on her cane. "My, you are a big one. No one's going to bother me, with you at my side. First thing to do is get you some clothes. That won't be hard, with all the empty houses around here. Then I'll pack, and we'll go to the station. I can buy the tickets, and you can carry my bags."

They found a cabin with clothing still in it, worn thin and faded. All the holes were mended and the clothes were clean and neatly folded, lying on a table, as if the people had almost taken them but gotten distracted or found they had no room. Brer Rabbit got himself a shirt and a pair of overalls. There were no shoes in the cabin. Shoes were expensive. No one would leave a pair of shoes behind.

"You'll have to go north barefoot," said Ma Johnson. "Won't do you any harm."

The body had hard feet, as if it was used to going barefoot; and Brer Rabbit himself had never worn shoes. He nodded. They moved on to Ma Johnson's house and packed her belongings.

She didn't have much for clothing, but a lot of strange things went in her suitcases: little bags and bottles; all kinds of twisted roots; and dolls no larger than his hand, made of fabric, with real human hair on their heads. They didn't look to him as if they were made for children. They had bead eyes that glinted in the lamplight and looked almost alive, as if there was someone inside, the way he was inside the clay man. Made him shiver, as he laid them in among Ma Johnson's shiny black dresses.

When they were finally done, they had two big suitcases, packed as full they could get and staying shut only because of straps.

"You take those," said Ma Johnson and picked up a carpet bag. "I'll take this and my cane."

Off they went. It was barely dawn. The air was cool. Mist hung in hollows and along the river they had to cross to get to town. Ma Johnson stumped ahead, moving briskly for a woman of her age. Brer Rabbit followed, his big arms straining to keep the suitcases up off the ground.

He was starting to have second thoughts about this journey. Ma Johnson said they were going to take a train north. He'd always stayed away from trains. They made too much commotion, puffing and hooting, shooting out sparks and smoke as their big iron wheels went click-clack across the countryside. He'd seen animals and people who'd been hit by them. It made an ugly mess.

"Can't we walk to Detroit?" he asked. His man legs were a lot longer than his rabbit legs had been. Surely he could go a long way with the stride he had now.

"I'm an old woman," Ma Johnson said.

"How about riding in a wagon?"

"Child, it's a long way north, and I want to get there before I die. We'll take the train."

Stump, stump over the bridge, mist drifting below them just above the river water. *Stump, stump* into the little town, still asleep, though there was a white man in the train station. The station master, Brer Rabbit decided, though he had never seen him before. As a rule, he stayed away from white folks.

Ma Johnson pulled an old beaded purse out of her carpet bag and bought two tickets.

"It seems like everyone's leaving," the white man said.

"Can't live on nothing," Ma Johnson said. "And nothing is what's left, since the weevils come."

The white man nodded, looking glum. Then he looked at Brer Rabbit. "I don't recollect seeing him before."

"My nephew," said Ma Johnson. "Folks call him Red."

"I can see why."

Brer Rabbit's body was clay red and so was his raggedy, badly cut hair. Even the irises of his eyes were as red as clay.

"You take good care of your auntie, boy."

Brer Rabbit didn't like the man's tone. He was used to respect, maybe not a lot, but some. Lack of it made him angry. That's what had gotten him into trouble with the tar baby.

There wasn't time to play a trick on the man, but he wanted to be rude to him, say something nasty. But something inside him was holding him back. It wasn't caution — he'd never had any. That promise he'd made to Ma Johnson must be working like a spell. He wasn't able to do anything that might cause her trouble.

"Yes, sir," he said to the white man.

They went outside and waited on the platform. The air smelled good to him: wood smoke and morning gardens, a distant hint of pine. This was home, and he was leaving it.

"What did you do to me?" he asked the old woman.

"You promised to help me get to Detroit. I made sure you will keep your promise, in spite of your nature. I know you, Brer Rabbit. You are a troublemaker and have always been one. But not anymore."

This was a frightening statement. But he didn't have time to think about it. The train arrived right then, rolling into the station, trailing clouds of smoke. It stopped, and steam hissed out around the big iron wheels. Brer Rabbit shivered. Ma Johnson climbed on board the black folks' car. After a moment, he followed, watching to be sure his bare feet didn't step in spit-out tobacco.

They found seats and settled in. The train gave a hoot and a jerk. Off they went, the train rumbling and swaying. It made Brer Rabbit a little queasy. But Ma Johnson had a jar of herb tea in her carpet bag. She opened it, and he took a swallow. That settled his stomach and made him less worried. It was good herb tea.

It was a long trip, and they had to change trains more than once. At first they ate the food in Ma Johnson's carpet bag. She had filled it with good home cooking, along with the herb tea. When the carpet bag was finally empty, they bought food at train stops. Ma Johnson had money, though he didn't know where. She kept it hidden and was careful about taking it out.

They slept on the train seats or on station benches. As they got farther north, the air got colder, though it was still summer or maybe early autumn. The plants along the tracks didn't look as lush as the plants back home. When the train stopped and he stood on the station platform, he smelled new aromas, sharper and thinner than the aromas down south, as if the air itself was getting an edge.

Two or three days along the way, Brer Rabbit noticed his skin was flaking. Little bits of clay fell on the train floor like dandruff.

"You're drying out," said Ma Johnson. "That clay isn't going to keep together."

"What can I do?" asked Brer Rabbit.

Ma Johnson sat and frowned. Finally she said, "Those train wheels are moving; and moving parts mean grease.

The next time there's a long stop, slip down between the cars. Find yourself some grease and slather it all over your body. That will moisten the clay."

"I'll have to take my clothes off," said Brer Rabbit.

"You been naked most of your life. It won't hurt you to be naked now."

Ma Johnson read the schedule and told him which stop would be long enough. When it came, Brer Rabbit got out and slid between two cars. Outside, in the flat fields of wherever they were, it was evening. Venus hung in the sky, as bright as could be, and there was a little sunset glow above the horizon. The station lamps were lit. So were lamps in the little town beyond the station. But there were plenty of shadows, especially between the cars. He could undress safely.

Did he want to do this? If he didn't, maybe the clay would flake all the way off. He'd be himself again. But he could feel the power of Ma Johnson's spell inside him, willing him to get her north. And he was a long way from home. How did he know if he'd be safe as a rabbit here? How did he know what the animals and people would be like?

In the end, he took off his clothes and slathered himself with train grease. It sank in, turning his skin black and shiny, going so deep that he couldn't feel it when he ran his hands over his bare arms and legs. There was just the feeling of skin, goose-bumped a little in the sharp evening air. Nothing slick or slippery at all. He rubbed grease in his hair as well. He didn't want it to be flaking and falling off. Then he climbed back into his clothes. The train hooted. He got back on the railroad car.

"My, that worked well," said Ma Johnson. "You fit right in now. You were a little bit too red before."

"Won't people notice that I've changed?"

"People notice what they want most of the time; and sometimes they notice what I want. I don't expect any trouble." She looked at him again. "Your eyes are dark. They turned the same color as your skin. Now, that is something I didn't expect. There's always something new in life, when a person pays attention; and it don't hurt to do magic. There's always something new to be found in magic."

He sat down next to the old woman. The car smelled of stale people. Mostly they were asleep, lolling as the train rocked: worn black folks in wrinkled clothing, holding what was precious to them and heading north. He felt less and less like himself.

They reached Detroit on a fall morning, when the sky was pale blue and cloudless, except for a few, high-up streaks of white. Coming into the city, Brer Rabbit could see trees starting to turn and lots of houses standing in rows. There were a few big buildings that might be factories, though he wasn't certain what a factory looked like.

The train station was stone and had the tallest rooms he had ever seen, going up and up to curved ceilings. Big windows let in wide beams of sunlight. The beams slanted down through dusty air till they reached the broad stone floor. He had never seen so much emptiness in a building. What for? The motes of dust dancing in the sunlight were pretty. But it was mighty expensive prettiness, as far as he could tell.

Most of the people in the station were white. They wore suits and hats and moved quickly, as if they had something important to do. The farther north they had come, the more people seemed to hurry.

Ma Johnson found a black shoeshine man and started a conversation with him. She was a great one for gathering information. Brer Rabbit stood by the suitcases and looked around at the stone floor, the stone walls, and the air that was partly in shadow and partly full of light and dancing dust. He listened to their conversation with half a rabbit ear. Ma Johnson was asking where the black folks lived and how to get there.

"It's called the Black Bottom," the shoeshine man said. "Though some folks call it Paradise Valley. I understand the first name, but not the second. You can find a rooming house there. Seems like the whole south is moving up here."

According to him, the stories Ma Johnson had heard were true: Mr. Henry Ford was hiring black folks at his Highland Park plant, and he treated them fairly.

She thanked the shoeshine man. Brer Rabbit picked up the suitcases and followed her out into the crisp fall air. It was then that he realized how really big the station was. He turned and craned his neck. It went up and up and up. He had to cross the street to count the stories. Eighteen of them, he made out. Why'd they build a train station like that? Did they have trains that flew?

The area around the station wasn't as built up as you'd expect. There were scattered buildings and empty lots, full of weeds. The people building the station had put it on the edge of town to allow for growth, the shoeshine man had told them. "White folks always expect growth. But it hasn't come. Not yet."

The street had rails. He wondered why, till he saw a little, one-car train run by.

"That's the trolley the shoeshine man was telling us about," Ma Johnson said. "We're gonna take one to the

Black Bottom. He gave me the name of a rooming house. Were you paying any attention?"

"Some."

There were automobiles as well. Brer Rabbit had seen a couple of these down south and more on the way north, but he wasn't used to them. They bounced past on their high, narrow wheels. Watching them, Brer Rabbit was reminded of the way Brer Spider picked his way through the underbrush on long, narrow legs, looking for something to eat or trick. No one could out-trick Brer Spider, not even Brer Rabbit.

"There is something about those things I don't like," Ma Johnson. "They give me a bad feeling, a shivering in the marrow of my bones. But the pay is good at Mr. Henry Ford's plant, and all you have to do is make the cars. You don't have to ride in one."

"Now, just a minute," Brer Rabbit said. "What makes you think I'm going to be hiring on with Mr. Henry Ford?"

"I need to get settled in, and that's going to take time," said Ma Johnson. "I spent almost all my money getting us here, and I won't be able to make more till people get to know me. Reputation matters a lot in the magic business. You can get a job right now."

"I promised to get you to Detroit," Brer Rabbit replied. "Here we are. I've kept my promise. I'm on my own now."

"What would you do instead of helping me?" Ma Johnson asked. "You have any idea how to get by in Detroit, Michigan?"

"I could go home," he said without conviction.

"Back to the weevils?"

He could feel her magic tugging at him. He had never lacked self-confidence; but he had never been in a place like this. His home was the pine woods, not a city full of houses and streets and white folks. The magic was tugging, and he was afraid.

"That's the story," the rabbit man said. It was getting on toward eight, and the bar was full of customers, people waiting for the music to begin. They'd both finished their dinners and a couple of drinks. Big Brown Mama had gotten herself a tiramisu dessert. The rabbit man made do with a decaf cappuccino.

"You can't stop there," Big Brown Mama said. "That was Detroit in nineteen-twenty-something, and this is Minneapolis in 2008. What happened in between?"

"There is more to the story," he admitted. "But if we stay here, we're going to hear jazz, which is fine by me. I like jazz. I'm not going talk through it. That's disrespectful and hard on my voice."

Big Brown Mama thought for a moment. She liked jazz too, and she wouldn't mind another glass of chardonnay. She certainly wasn't going to let the rabbit man get away. "Why'd you address me out on the street?" she asked.

"You're a good looking woman," the rabbit man said. "But that wasn't the reason. Something about you told me we'd get along. You might understand me. Most people don't. All they see is the man, not the rabbit; and the rabbit is what I really am. Don't ask me why I felt that way."

She didn't need to ask. It was her Big Mama personality, the linen skirt that didn't wrinkle, the dangling and flashing galaxies. Magic calls to magic, and he was the most magiced-up person she'd seen in a while.

Another glass of chardonnay and some music sounded fine. From the look of the old black man testing the piano, the music was going to be good. The rest of the trio was white and young. But she had a lot of hope for the old man. He had the look of authority.

They stayed though two sets. The trio played fifties modern jazz, as crisp and clean as an air conditioner cranked up high. It was a fine thing to hear on a hot summer evening.

The old man was as good as she had hoped, playing his piano as delicately and precisely as a surgeon operating on a brain, his big, knobby fingers like scalpels on the keys. She was pretty sure this was a mixed metaphor, but she didn't care.

Big Brown Mama had two more glasses of wine. But she had no trouble as she swayed out on her high heels like an old-time movie star.

"Can we meet again?" the rabbit man asked, standing on the hot sidewalk.

"You bet," replied Big Brown Mama. "Give me your number, and I'll give you a call."

"Can't I call you?" the man asked.

"I'm going out of town."

He looked reluctant for a moment, then gave her a number, which she memorized. It was a good number. He hadn't made it up. He was too lonely to risk not seeing her again.

They parted, shaking hands because they didn't know what else to do. The rabbit man walked off along Nicollet Mall, and Big Brown Mama stepped from Minneapolis in 2008 to the end of the twenty-second century. As I mentioned, the Big People can stroll up and down the arrow of time. More than that, they can step over centuries.

The twenty-first century was about to go sour, and she preferred to stay on the other side of the bad times. There was a resort on the moon she liked. It had just been opened and was still brand spanking new, at the edge of the lunar colony with a good view of Earth, hanging above sharp mountains like a blue and white marble.

She picked up her luggage, left in a locker at the rocket terminal, and rode a sliding walkway to the hotel. Mostly she was in tunnels. But once she crossed a dome carpeted with green grass. A small flock of sheep trimmed the grass. One or two had reproduced. A pair of young lambs frolicked around their staid seniors, bounding way up, then floating gently down like feathers, obviously comfortable with the lunar gravity. Flowers from Earth rose to surprising heights and opened enormous blossoms.

She knew there were still plenty of problems on Earth: mountains without glaciers and drowned coastal cities, vast areas of desert and pollution, dead spots in the ocean. But the worst was past. Humanity was fixing their home and moving into space. These were big projects and worth doing, unlike many human activities. Big Brown Mama liked upbeat eras.

She signed into the hotel. A robot took her bags to her room. She changed and went to swim in the hotel pool, where she blew the minds of numerous men and several women. Imagine a creamy brown woman in a moon-white bathing suit that left nothing to anyone's imagination. She walked gracefully along the pool's edge, watching the waves that moved slowly down it, generated by a machine at one end. There was something about big, tall lunar waves, cresting and curling over in amazing slow motion, that really appealed to her. Big Brown Mama dove in and sported like a dolphin.

She slept well in her mesh bed, held safely against the risk of accidental falling, not that she'd be hurt in this G. In the morning she ate a modest breakfast, then took a tour of the colony, which was growing rapidly. She liked progress. It was so much more cheery than collapse.

Big Brown Mama stayed at the hotel for two more days, then got her clothing cleaned, repacked it, and deposited her luggage in a locker. In one quick step, she was back in Minneapolis at the start of the twenty-first century.

It was another hot day, with haze obscuring big, white clouds that were probably going to turn into thunderheads. Even though she was wearing her linen suit that did not wrinkle, she felt sticky. She checked her watch and discovered it was Sunday, 3 p.m., late August 2008. (The watch picked up signals from the nearest atomic clock, which mean it always gave the local time accurately.) The rabbit man wasn't likely to be at work, if he had a job, which she didn't know. She got out her cell phone and punched in his number.

He answered, and they made a date. She wanted to hear the rest of his story, and she thought she really ought to help him, if he still wanted to be free of his human body. The Big Mamas and Poppas could be self-indulgent and arbitrary, when they felt like it, but they also had a sense of *noblesse oblige*.

They met in St. Paul, at a coffee shop near the river. There was a fireplace, with the fire turned off since it was summer still, and a lot of faux North Woods decor: rough stone and pine logs and footstools in the shape of bears.

The place felt comforting. She had been in the Twin Cities too long, if faux North Woods looked good to her.

They got fancy coffee drinks and sat down in front of the turned-off fireplace. Big Brown Mama kicked off her impossibly high heels and put her feet up on the nearest bear. Ah, that felt good!

"What happened next?" she asked the rabbit man. Today he was wearing jeans and work boots and a plain blue tee-shirt.

He sipped the coffee, getting a foam mustache, which he wiped off. "Ma Johnson found a place to rent, and I got a job at the Highland Park plant. Let me tell you, that work was hard. I wasn't the only man having trouble. Cotton farming is brutal, but you don't punch a time clock, and you don't have to stay in one place, doing the same thing over and over, not taking a break to swallow water or pee, unless the foreman says it's okay. There's nothing natural about an assembly line, and not everyone—even good, hard workers, men who could hoe or chop cotton all day in the hot sun—could learn to do that kind of work. I could, which was surprising. When I was Brer Rabbit, I never stayed put, and I never kept to any task, unless I was making trouble.

"It must have been her magic made me clock in every day." He set down his fancy coffee drink and folded his big, work-hardened hands. "We stayed in a boarding house first. Then we found an apartment, and she set up her business in the front room. She hung curtains over the windows, so the room was dark, and got furniture. At first it was cheap, and she draped pieces of cloth over it, so folks couldn't see how shabby it was. But when I could afford it, she bought good hardwood. She liked hardwood. If you took care of it and polished it well, you could see the life of the tree shining out. 'It's still in there,' she told me, running her old hand over a chair or table. 'The sunlight and water and the way leaves glitter when the wind moves them on a hot, bright day. All held in the wood.'

"I don't know if she was right. But I know there's something mighty taking about a good, well polished piece of hardwood.

"There were lamps in the room, oil at first. She liked the way the light flickered, making the eyes of her dolls gleam and blink. She had them set out everywhere, and they made my skin crawl. Either she moved them around, or they moved on their own. I'd go in that room, and their beady eyes would be shining at me from a new place, as if they'd climbed up on the mantel or gathered together in a chair for some kind of convocation. I don't know what she did with them, and I didn't want to know. I stayed away from that room as much as I could.

"People came, once she got handbills made and hired boys to take them around the Bottom. 'Madam Johnson, Advisor.' That's what the handbills said.

"I was working my ass off on Ford's assembly line, and she was telling people what numbers to play and selling them potions to cure their illnesses or keep their men. I could never make up my mind about what she did. She could do magic. I knew that for a fact. Though it was an up-and-down kind of magic. Sometime it worked, and sometimes it didn't. 'What I do is natural,' she said to me. 'And nature ain't reliable. You ought to know that. One year your crop is good. The next year the weevils come. But nature is powerful, Red. You remember that.'"

He glanced at Big Brown Mama and smiled. "People asked me how I got a nickname like Red, seeing as how I was black as the ace of spades. I said it was childhood foolery, but I was stuck with it.

"Those potions of hers did work part of the time; and they were cheaper than a doctor, if you could find a doctor to treat you; and it wasn't modern medicine in those days, even if a white man did it. Mostly, it was witchcraft and butchery, same as Ma Johnson, except she didn't cut people up. If you were a poor black woman and you had cancer, Ma Johnson might be as good anything else you could find.

"I saw people get well and win at numbers, using her advice and the herbs she gave them. I saw other people lose at numbers and die."

He unfolded his hands and took another sip of the fancy coffee drink. "I never played the numbers. It's a fool's game. Turned out I had a gift for cards, so I played them, and hung out in low dives and blind pigs. Drank too much and listened to good music. Found out about human women. You may not believe it, but I wasn't much of a womanizer back when I was a rabbit. But I did enjoy women, once I found out about them.

"There were a couple I liked enough so I thought of settling down. But how could I? I wasn't really a man. I was a rabbit. And I had Ma Johnson to look after. I think she kept a spell on me, to make me care about her and to make me keep working on that damn assembly line.

"I don't think I ever would have settled down far enough to marry. I knew men in the plant steady as rocks, deacons at their churches, who worked themselves hard as mules to provide for their families. But I had Brer Rabbit inside me, and he was never reliable. I guess I was doing those women a favor by never getting serious.

"We stayed in Detroit till I got a job at the Rouge plant in Dearborn, Michigan. It was Henry Ford's biggest plant, the biggest plant of its kind in the world. He had a fleet of ships on the Great Lakes, and they'd bring coal and iron and limestone from Minnesota and northern Michigan and Ohio. The raw materials went in one end of the plant, and Ford cars came out the other. That plant did everything.

"I was a tool-and-die worker by then and making good money. It's the best job in a car plant, and no one but Henry Ford would let a black man do it. Not in those days. I've heard a lot of stories about him. How he hated Jews and was a little bit too friendly with Adolph Hitler. How he hired gangsters to fight the union. But he was a friend to black folks, when we needed one badly."

"People are complicated," Big Brown Mama said and flipped one of her galaxy earrings. Fortunately it was an uninhabited galaxy. No one was hurt.

"I suppose you're right," the rabbit man said. "I bought a house in Inkster, which is right next to Dearborn. Black folks could buy there, when they couldn't buy in most other places. The way I heard it, Henry Ford established Inkster for the black workers at River Rouge. The white folks lived in Dearborn. She—Ma Johnson—brought her magic business with her and set it up in the front parlor of my house. The lamps were electric instead of oil, and the drapes were real red velvet. It cost a lot, but she wanted real velvet. There were oriental carpets—real ones—on the floor, and the furniture was antiques out of the nineteenth century. The furniture didn't cost much. Most folks wanted modern things, made in the twentieth century. But

Ma Johnson liked old things and old ways, and she didn't change much about her working room. It was still full of shadows, and the dolls still sat and lay everywhere, their bead eyes gleaming and winking. They always looked mean to me, and they got meaner-looking as she got older.

"She'd been straight as a rake when I first knew her. But time bent her over, till she was like a willow branch in an ice storm. Down south her cane had been mostly for show and to wave at animals and children if they bothered her. Now she needed it, half for support and half to feel her way, as her eyes got dimmer. As old as she was, she kept living right through the hard times in the thirties and the union struggles and the war; and I kept right on working.

"I was never laid off, which was mostly luck and the fact that Henry Ford could trust his black workers to side with him and not with the union. I'm not proud of it, but I crossed a picket line in 1934. We knew Henry Ford was our friend, and we weren't certain about the white folks in the union. A lot of them came from the south, and they brought their opinions with them. I can't say the white folks from the north were any better. The only people you could trust were the Communists. They believed in solidarity, and they believed in it hard. Except for them — well, most white folks have always been willing to put skin color first and side with the bosses and landlords against us. So why should we side with them, when they were down and out and trying to organize?

"In the end, we joined. But that's not the story I'm telling."

"Did you ever try to get free of her?" Big Brown Mama asked.

He nodded. "I asked her to get me out of this body more than once. After she was settled and had set up her business, she agreed to try, and I think she did try, though I can't be sure. Every time she began her work, I'd go under — fall asleep or unconscious; and then I'd wake up, and I'd be the same as before. Still a man." He made a face. "I don't know what I would have done, if she had turned me into a rabbit. Hopped back to Georgia? Or hid out in a vacant lot? Maybe I'd've been able to survive in the park on Belle Isle. In the end, she told me she couldn't do it. The grease and clay had set like concrete. She couldn't break through.

"She might have been telling the truth about my body. But I think she put more than one spell on me, and the one that made me stay in Inkster and work a steady job might have come off, if she'd been willing to take it off. But she didn't want to grow old and die alone. It isn't easy for a magic woman to make friends. I can't say that she had any. Not real ones, the kinds who'll sit with you when you're sick or dying.

"I didn't notice she was failing till the war. I was too old to be drafted, and I wasn't about to volunteer. Rabbits don't fight wars. So I stayed in Detroit at the Rouge Plant. A hundred and twenty thousand men worked at River Rouge during the war, making airplanes and tanks. Detroit was the arsenal of democracy. That's what they called it.

"By the end of the war, she was almost blind. That's what killed her. She was struck down by a 1948 Ford F-1 pickup truck while crossing a street in Inkster; and she was dead before I reached the hospital. I sat with her a while: a stiff, thin, old black lady lying in a bed. I have never felt lonelier.

"I suppose it was a good end: sudden and soon over. But it didn't make me feel any better.

"I buried her. A few people came to the funeral, because they were curious. As I said, a witch doesn't have a lot of friends.

"Then I went home to the house in Inkster. It was a bright day in October, with the leaves golden-yellow and starting to fall. I took all her magic tools out to the back yard and buried them in a leaf pile and burnt the pile. I swear to heaven those little dolls were crying and cursing me as they burned. No one else heard them, and I told myself I had imagined the sound. I had to do it. I couldn't leave her magic lying around for fools to pick up and try. It was too strong and dangerous.

"That wasn't enough to free me. I stayed in the house and at my job. I think her spells still had a hold on me, though I started to take trips, either to Chicago, because the blues were so good there, or up to Idlewild. That was a fancy Negro resort in the northern part of the Lower Peninsula. Well-to-do black folks stayed there, back in the days when they couldn't stay at white resorts. I was a working man, but I was well paid, and I could afford to go.

"I wasn't interested in spending time with high-tone people. My friends in the plant suited me just fine. But Idlewild got all the best black performers. I liked seeing them; and I liked the forest. It wasn't southern pine, but it was pine. I'd go out alone and take a deep breath. My whole head would fill with the smell of pine. I'd close my eyes and hear the needles hiss and whisper, as the branches moved in the wind, and imagine being Brer Rabbit again." He finished his fancy coffee drink, got up and ordered a new one, then returned to the chair next to Big Brown Mama. Sitting down again, he put his feet on the next bear. "I always ended by going back to Inkster and my job in the plant, till the time I met Nanabozho.

"I was up at Idlewild and out in the woods, standing there, listening to the trees and smelling the pine smell— All at once, someone said in a big, deep voice, 'Who are you, cousin?'

"I turned around. There was a man standing ten feet away, big and dark with long, black hair in braids. He had on work pants and a flannel shirt, lumberjack boots and a black hat with a broad brim. There were rabbit ears sticking up through the crown of the hat.

"'Who are you?' I asked in reply.

"'My name is Nanabozho, if that means anything.'

"It didn't. I shook my head.

"The damnest thing happened. He began to flicker, like cottonwood leaves in the sunlight on a windy day. One moment, he looked like a man with rabbit ears; and the next moment he was something strange in between a man and rabbit, man-shaped, but covered with fur and with a buck-tooth rabbit face; and then he shrank down till he was rabbit-sized and rabbit-shaped; and then he swelled up again into a man.

"'Can you do that?' he asked.

"'No,' I said.

"'You should be able to. I can see you're another person like me.'"

"'I'm stuck like this,' I said.

"'Come to my camp. I've got coffee there. We can sit and talk.'

"So we did. The camp was by a stream farther back in the forest: a little fire that produced almost no smoke, a bedroll, and a backpack. A couple of narrow beams of sunlight came down through the trees and danced around as the pine branches moved, making the blue enamel coffee pot next to the fire gleam. He made coffee and a pan of corn bread. We drank and ate, and I told my story.

"'I can see you in there, under all that clay and grease,' Nanabozho said. 'There's got to be a way to get you out. Maybe if I take hold of your rabbit ears—' He grabbed at the air above my head and pulled. Let me tell you, it hurt! I felt as if my ears—my human ears—were being pulled off the sides of my head, and my brain was being pulled out through the top of my head. I shouted as loudly as I could, and he let go. 'I thought I could yank you out of there, but maybe I can't.' He poked my chest. 'It's solid. I don't think I can dig through there.'

"'Don't even try,' I said.

"'I've got a good Bowie knife—'

"I jumped up. He laughed. 'It's just a joke, cousin. A knife would do no good against all that concrete. I'd have to take a sledge hammer to you.'

"'Are you crazy?' I asked and took several steps back. He was a big man, strong looking and not in his right mind, I was beginning to think.

"'It's another joke.'

"'You joke too much,' I said.

"'I'm a trickster and a joker,' he answered. 'So are you, though it looks to me as if you've lost your sense of humor. I think you should come and visit my grandmother.'

"The man part of me wanted to stay where I was or go back to the resort. Louis Armstrong was playing that night. I didn't think he'd ever beat the work he did as a young man, but he was still a fine horn player, and I didn't want to miss a note.

"The rabbit part of me was more of a risk taker. I remembered that. No one could tell Brer Rabbit what to do or when to be careful. I looked Nanabozho over. No question he was big and looked strong. Well, I was good-sized and strong as all those years on the line could make me. I thought I could fight him, if I had to. Anyway, those rabbit ears sticking through his hat looked friendly.

"'Who's your grandmother?' I asked.

"'Her name is Nokomis. My mother died giving birth. After she was gone, my grandmother found me as a clot of blood and raised me as a rabbit.'

"'Found you as a clot of blood.'

"Nanabozho grinned. 'That's what she told me.'

"'And raised you as a rabbit? Why?'

"'You can ask her, if you want.'

"That got the rabbit part curious, and nothing ever stopped Brer Rabbit once he was curious. I said, 'I'll go with you.'

"He put out his fire and packed his camp, and we set out. It was a long hike. The sun got low, and it was dark under the pine trees. The man part told me I was a fool. The rabbit part said, 'You sure have gotten timid. All that clay on you has put out your fire, and all that grease has made you want to slide through life like Brer Snake, never lifting your head.'

"Let me tell you, it's hard to listen to insults from yourself."

Big Brown Mama laughed and nodded, though she never insulted herself. She had too much self-respect.

"We finally got to a clearing full of tall grass. The pine forest stood all around, dark and shadowy. Above the clearing the sky was still blue, and a horn-moon hung in it. A tar paper shack stood in the middle of the clearing, leaning to one side with a tree branch propping it up. There was one window with no glass and lamplight shining out. The door hung half open. A path led through the grass to it.

"'This place needs work,' I told Nanabozho. 'You ought to give your grandmother some help. That door needs to be rehung, and you ought to put a screen on that window. The poor woman's going to be et alive by bugs.'

"Nanabozho grinned. 'She likes it this way. The bugs don't bother her. Not the mosquitoes, not the deer flies, not even the no-see-ums. She's a woman of strong character and stronger abilities. Come in.'

"We pushed the door all the way open. Inside was a room full of clutter. I can't describe it any better. It was harder seeing in there than in my front parlor, even though a kerosene lamp burned on a table. I thought I saw a rack of antlers on the wall, and a fur thrown over the back of a chair. But the antlers moved, and a deer was looking at me. The fur rose up on its hind legs and turned into something like a big weasel. It glared at me with mean, black eyes.

"'Be polite,' said an old, old voice. The weasel-thing settled down and became a fur again.

"There was a woman sitting at the table. She was the one who'd spoken. She was tiny and withered, covered with wrinkles, with white hair in braids. Older than Ma Johnson. But when she lifted her head, her eyes were sharp. 'How'd you get inside that body?' she asked. 'It can't be good for you, being all covered with clay and grease. I bet you have trouble breathing.'

"I tried to take a deep breath and realized she was right. All these years, and I hadn't realized how much I was being stifled.

"The woman got up, leaning on a cane, and hobbled over to me. She peered up and down. 'I saw my grandson in a clot of blood and managed to shape the clot, so it became Nanabozho. But I don't think I can do the same for you.' She made a fist and knocked on my chest. It was a strong blow, surprising from a woman so old and small. I took a step back. 'That clay is rock solid hard,' Nokomis said. 'The clot of blood that became Nanabozho was soft.' Tilting her head, she looked up at me. 'A powerful witch did this, using a kind of magic I don't understand; and I'm not sure how much she understood it, either.

"'That clay is like mud, and that's what the world is made from. Muskrat brought it up from the bottom of the water, back when everything was covered with water. We'd all be swimming except for him. There was magic in the mud, which is why it was possible to make the world out of it; and there's still a little magic left in all the world's mud and dirt and clay.

"'I think your witch used the magic in clay to give you a man's body. But then she added grease, and that comes from machinery. It's industrial magic, white people's magic; and I'm not sure I know how to handle it.' She stood for several moments, leaning on her cane and frowning. The antlers on the wall behind her tilted and looked down at me with soft, dark, deer eyes. The skin on the chair rose up and looked mean.

"'When in doubt, build a sweat lodge,' she said finally. 'We'll try to sweat you out of that man-shape.'

"'That's a good idea, Grandmother,' Nanabozho said. 'You come with me, cousin. We'll build a lodge. There's nothing that isn't made better by sweating.'

"It wasn't hard work. There was a lodge out back, half falling down like the tar paper house. It was round and not even as tall as I was, made of saplings bent over and fastened together, then covered with strips of birch bark. The bark was old and half rotten, gone in places, curling in other places, with green patches of moss growing on it.

"'We'll patch the roof with canvas,' Nanabozho said. 'It'll take too long to gather birch bark. And I'd better be sure those branches are solid.' He ducked into the lodge, and I heard him moving around. The lodge shook a little: Nanabozho testing the branches. Finally, he came out. 'It'll hold.'

"'I don't mean to be rude,' I said. 'But why is everything so run down?'

"'My grandmother doesn't like change. Old people get that way. You can kill an old person by fixing up her home, just like you can kill a young person by sending him off to a government school. It's a good idea to be careful about improvement. White people aren't, which is one of their problems.'

"That didn't make a lot of sense to me, so I kept quiet. We let the lodge be that evening, since the last light was fading out of the sky, and the clearing was dark. Nanabozho built a campfire, and we camped out. There wasn't room in the house for us, which didn't bother me one bit. The animal skin on the chair made me nervous.

"We ate dinner with Nokomis, sitting at the rickety table in the dim light of the kerosene lamp. She served a venison stew and wild rice casserole. Good food, though

I don't eat a lot of meat. It seemed to fit with this evening and place.

"After I'd been sitting for a while, I realized there was something under the table. Given that house, with the antlers that had eyes and the skin that could rear up on the hind legs it didn't have, I got nervous and looked down quickly. A pair of ducks sat comfortably among our feet.

""There are ducks under the table,' I said.

"Nanabozho nodded. '*Aninishib* in our language. The mallard duck in yours. You ought to know them. They get everywhere, like mice.'

"I nodded.

"Nanabozho went on. 'That's one reason Grandmother keeps her door open. She has a lot of friends, who come to visit.'

"The ducks waddled out from under the table. The female was brown and spotted. The male had a green head that shone, even in the cabin's dim light. Nanabozho fed them pieces of fried bread.

"Then we all slept, Nokomis in her house, the two of us by the camp fire. The ducks came out and joined us, sleeping at the edge of the firelight. Nanabozho was right about the bugs. The woods should have been full of them, but I didn't hear or feel one all night. I did hear other things thrashing in the undergrowth. Maybe raccoons. Maybe bears or wolves. I didn't know what lived there, aside from ducks.

"In the morning, we fixed the lodge, and Nanabozho built a fire outside. 'Nothing goes in the fire that isn't sacred,' he told me. 'Wood, sage, sweet grass, and tobacco. No gasoline or newspaper or any other kind of crap. Then we heat rocks, and then the rocks go in the lodge.'

"I helped him as best I could. The longer I've been a man, the stranger the world seems. This fellow was nothing like the folks I'd known down south, and nothing like the folks in Detroit, and I didn't know where I was with him or his grandmother.

"When the rocks were hot he carried them into the lodge with a pitchfork. There was a pit in the middle. The rocks went in there, and a bucket of water beside them. Then we stripped down and went inside, naked as the day we were born. Though I can't say I remember being born or ever hearing about Brer Rabbit's birth. Maybe there was a story. No one ever told it to me.

"We sat down. There was light coming in through cracks and holes, so I could see at first. Then he poured water on the rocks. Steam rose hissing, and the lodge filled with clouds. It was like being in a thick fog, except the fog was hot and smelled of vegetation. Nanabozho was putting leaves on the hot, wet stones. I could see that much.

"'Sage and sweet grass, cedar and tobacco. Only sacred things,' he told me again.

"Sweat poured off me; and when I took that hot, moist air into my lungs, things began to happen. I could feel myself begin to change. At first it felt good. I was sweating out Detroit—the dirt and grease and oil, the bad air, the bone-breaking hard work, the white-folk meanness. Even at Henry Ford's plant, with Mr. Ford laying down the law and saying black folks should be treated fairly, there was a lot of meanness.

"All that was pouring out of me, running down my black skin like a river. I was sweating anger and fear, despair and bone-tiredness, losing all the bad times I'd had as a man. The trouble was, I was sweating myself away. I felt it first in my hands and looked down. My fingers were no longer separate, my hands no longer shaped like hands. Instead, they had turned into blobs of greasy black clay. I should have seen Brer Rabbit's paws coming through the clay. But I didn't.

"I lifted an arm. I could still do that, though I could no longer move my fingers. The flesh on the arm sagged. At first it seemed as if it was slipping off the bone. Then, as I watched, the bones of that arm began to bend, pulled down by the weight of my sagging flesh.

I was melting like the witch in *The Wizard of Oz*—all of me, bones as well as flesh, the black man outside and Brer Rabbit inside.

"'This ain't right,' I said to Nanabozho.

"He looked at me, frowning. 'Take a deep breath and try to pull yourself free. You're a rabbit, not a man.'

"I tried. I breathed in and thought, I ain't a black auto worker from Detroit. I'm a trickster rabbit from the pine woods. That's the real me.

"But it didn't work. I kept melting, my belly sagging like an old man's belly, my thighs sliding down till my legs were bone-thin and my feet were huge and swollen. Brer Rabbit wasn't coming out, but I was going away. I could see what lay ahead: a black pool of grease and clay, laying on the sweat lodge floor. 'I'm going to die here,' I said to Nanabozho.

"He stood up and grabbed a towel. 'I need to talk to my grandmother. You stay here.'

"I had to—I couldn't walk. My shoulders were sinking into my chest, and my neck couldn't hold the weight of my head. It sagged forward, my chin going right into my breastbone. What a way to end!

"All at once Nokomis was in the lodge. She picked up the bucket of water and poured it over me. It should have been ordinary water, maybe a little warm, but it felt like ice. I could feel myself getting solid.

""That's better,' she said. 'Though you are still a mess.' She prodded my chest. 'Nice and soft, like Nanabozho was when he was born. I can shape you now. But not in here. Nanabozho, get a blanket and wrap him in it. I want him carried out into the clearing, and I don't want any pieces to fall off.'

"Nanabozho did as he was told. I did nothing, afraid to move. He laid me in the clearing under a clear, blue, early afternoon sky. Sunlight flooded down around me. Nokomis knelt beside me and pulled the blanket back.

"Her little, thin hands began to work me over, molding me like a piece of wet clay. That's about all I was by then. She punched and pulled and smoothed, singing all the time in a low voice. I didn't understand the words. The song wasn't in English.

"I lay there, dozing and dreaming a little. I knew I was in a forest clearing, alone except for Nokomis and Nanabozho. But it seemed to me I was on a dance ground. Nanabozho was beating on a big drum; and four women danced around me, wearing Indian dresses with metal cones sewn on. One dress was red as blood; one was snow-white; one was deep blue-black like night in the country; and one was sun-yellow. The metal cones on their dresses flashed and rattled as they moved to the drum's slow, deep beat. They were Indian women with brown skins and long, black hair; and I have to say they were beautiful. Though the most beautiful thing about the dream was old Nokomis, shaping me back into a man.

"I'd sooner be a rabbit, but I didn't want to be nothing. Being nothing was worse than being in Detroit.

"My dream ended, and I was back in the clearing. Nokomis was standing over me, wiping her old hands against one another. I was my human self again.

"'Well, that didn't work. Maybe it's because you aren't an Indian,' Nokomis said. 'A sweat is supposed to get everything bad out of you. But there should be something left after.'

"'Maybe I've lost the rabbit,' I answered bitterly. 'Maybe there's nothing left of me but grease and clay.'

"Nokomis shook her head. 'The rabbit is in there. But he's so mixed up in the clay and grease and man-ness that I can't see a way to get him free. I don't know what kind of magic might work. You can't sweat him out, and the healing dance did nothing except heal you of melting. It didn't heal you of being a man.'

"'There was a dance?' I asked.

"She nodded. 'You saw the dancers. They are relatives of mine, and they do a very good healing dance. They helped me shape you back into a man, but they couldn't free the rabbit, any more than the sweat could. I don't think this is an Indian problem.'

"It was too late for me to go back to Idlewild, so I stayed another night in the clearing.

"'I'm sorry,' Nanabozho told me. 'I thought my grandmother could get you free.'

"I sat for a while and paid attention to my body and mind. 'I think a lot of bad things got sweated out of me. For one thing, I'm quitting work when I get back, and I'm moving out of Detroit. Nothing holds me there; and I feel a lot cleaner up here. I came from pine woods. These woods aren't the same, but there is something about the smell of any kind of pine. Even if I'm a man, I can live where there is forest.'

"Nanabozho nodded and looked up at the sky. I followed his gaze. Stars blazed over the clearing, as bright as a car plant lit up for the night shift, all the windows pouring out light. But the stars were far prettier than any car plant, even the ones designed by the famous architect Albert Kahn.

"Nothing in this world is prettier than stars.

"He led me back to Idlewild the next day. I packed and went home to Inkster and put my house up for sale. It sold quickly. These were the rich days after the war, when everyone was looking to buy housing. I cleaned out the house and sold what I could at a yard sale. What I couldn't sell, I threw out or gave away.

"When that was done, I gave two weeks' notice at the plant and headed north with nothing except one suitcase and a checkbook. One thing you have to say about car plants. The pay is good.

"I say I headed north. First I went to Chicago, which was pretty much due west. I was tired of factory work. I found a job at a blues club, mopping floors. It was a lot easier than making cars, and I got to listen to the music. The club was in a rough neighborhood on the South Side. After I broke up a couple of fights, the boss made me a bouncer. From there, I worked up to bartender. Most of the customers liked beer or whiskey, so I didn't have to learn a lot of fancy drinks. Now and then, some white folks came in and wanted something special. As white folks went, they weren't bad. The only thing that would bring white folks into that part of town was a deep-down love of blues. They came politely, on their best behavior. If I couldn't make their drinks, they smiled and drank beer.

"When there was a fight I broke it up; and I listened to the blues. This was big city blues, not the music I had listened to down south. It was harder and louder, the way people get in a city.

"I didn't intend to stay in Chicago. I just stopped for a while to listen to the music. After a few years, I headed north to Minneapolis. I knew they had pine woods in Minnesota, good fishing in the lakes and rivers, and Indians. Since Ma Johnson died, only two people had looked at me and seen the person I really was: Nanabozho and Nokomis.

"A funny thing! There's a lake in Minneapolis named for Nokomis. But the people here don't know anything about her. After I found that out, I tracked down the poetry that Henry Wadsworth Longfellow wrote about Nokomis. It's called *The Song of Hiawatha*. He got pretty much everything wrong. Well, that's to be expected. Joel Chandler Harris got me wrong. White people don't listen as well as they should."

"That's true," said Big Brown Mama, remembering one of her relatives, a termite-white Big Poppa. That man had no more sense than an insect, and he didn't listen any better than insects did. You want a termite to pay attention, you have to use a pheromone.

"I've been here ever since," the rabbit man said. "I don't seem to age much, though I don't feel as limber as I used to. When I first came, there weren't a lot of black folks. Most were in St. Paul, because of the railroads. Those were good jobs, though the white workers didn't want us in their unions; so we organized our own. Most failed, but the

Porters Union lasted. People think now that it was humbling to work as a Pullman porter. I knew a lot of those porters in St. Paul. They were hard working, educated, thoughtful men. A porter recruited Martin Luther King to the civil rights movement, and A. Phillip Randolph, the president of the union, helped organize the 1963 Civil Rights March. Bayard Rustin did the actual work; but A. Phillip Randolph called in every debt he was owed after thirty years in the union movement. You can say a lot of things about A. Phillip Randolph, both good and bad, but that march was something."

"Did you go?" Big Brown Mama asked.

"You bet. I rode a union bus down from St. Paul. When we got close to Washington, we were in a line of buses, a lot of them with union banners on their sides. That was A. Phillip Randolph's doing.

"There were black folks standing by the highway, holding on to their kids and watching the buses roll in one after another. When we got into the city, folks were standing on their porches. I can still remember how they looked—solemn and waiting. Something important was happening. They didn't know if it was going to work. They weren't cheering or smiling. But they wanted their kids to see the buses. They wanted to hope and believe.

"I'm a rabbit, but I'm also a man. That day I was proud to be a man, but also sad. What those folks were waiting for was not going to happen yet, no matter what the Rev. Dr. Martin Luther King Jr. said in his famous speech."

He was right about this. History was a long haul, and only people who lived as long as Big Brown Mama saw the result. Most folk saw the fight and the small gains and the setbacks. They didn't see the cities on the moon.

"Anyway, I lived in St. Paul, even after they put an interstate highway right through Rondo, the old black neighborhood. That happened in the 1960s, the same time as the big march. There are times I think white people are like weevils. They'll drive you from your home. The weevils did it because they wanted to eat, and the white folks did it because they wanted an easy ride to work.

"They scattered us all over St. Paul, the way the weevils had scattered us all over the middle of the country. The community was never the same.

"I wonder sometimes, did we lose more than we gained in the sixties? Those were great days. We got the vote, and maybe we finally got into American society, instead of always being at the edges and in the shadows.

"But those big highway machines smashed through our homes, and the good jobs we'd fought for and won — on the railroads, in the factories and mills — mostly vanished, just vaporized, gone from one decade to the next. I went to Detroit a few years back. There's block after block with no houses, just empty lots full of tall weeds, the way it was when they were putting up the city and planning big for the future. Only this time they're tearing it down. I saw skyscrapers — big tall buildings, that railway station I saw when I first arrived — all boarded up. How can you board up a skyscraper and leave it? A famous building that used to be full of sunlight and steam?

"How many times can black folks look at ruin and pull ourselves together and begin again?"

Big Brown Mama had no answer to this question.

"I'd done all the steady work I ever wanted to do in Detroit, and I was good with machinery, so I became a handyman. People said I had magic hands. Maybe I do. Maybe that railroad grease gave me something special.

"I did pick-up work, took a job when I wanted one, left it when I wanted to loaf or travel—down to Mexico, off to Paris. There was some good jazz in Paris. Then I'd come back to St. Paul, and then I'd leave again. I had friends, including women friends; but they couldn't see the rabbit in me, which meant they never really saw me. I suppose I was lonely." He looked lonely, sitting with his big, worn hands folded around the coffee mug—as if he wanted to hold something else, a person who wasn't there.

"Did you ever meet Nanabozho again?" Big Brown Mama asked.

"We meet up north to go fishing. I've done other things with him, ricing and sugaring, even some hunting and trapping. But mostly we fish. There's nothing better than pulling a good-sized fish out a lake with the air smelling of pine and water, and no one around except him and me.

"Some of the folks on the reservations know who he is. Old folks, mostly. They can see his ears, but not mine."

Did the rabbit man sound sad?

"Well, said Big Brown Mama. "That's quite a story. I suspect, from what I've heard, that you are an archetype and a genuine American myth, embodying much that is important about this country. Someone like that shouldn't be trapped inside a middle-aged black man. Fortunately for you, I have many abilities. Even Nokomis isn't up to my speed."

The rabbit man's just barely visible ears flicked back and forth. "Can you free me?"

"I can surely try. Give me some thinking time." She stood up and smoothed her dress. This time it was sun-yellow linen, with nary a wrinkle after she ran her hands down the fabric. Her earrings were green nebulae with stars shining inside them. You couldn't find anything finer on the NASA Hubble picture site.

"I could go back in time and change your story, so you never became a man or went to Detroit."

"Wouldn't I forget what's happened to me?"

"No, because it would never have happened. You can't remember a branch of time that's been cut off. It doesn't exist. It's as gone as the factories in Detroit and the steel mills in Gary, except those left scars and empty places. This would leave nothing. You'd be Brer Rabbit in the Georgia pine woods. You'd never know anything else."

The man considered, frowning, then shook his head. "I don't want to forget Detroit and Chicago and Rondo. I don't even want to forget Ma Johnson. A man is what he's done and what he remembers."

He was going to have to decide if he was a rabbit or a man, Big Brown Mama thought. But this wasn't her concern. If she could get him free, he'd have a choice. She touched one of the ghostly ears. It shivered. She tugged it. The man grimaced.

"Let's go take a walk by the river," she said. "The people here are going to think I'm crazy, pulling at something that isn't there."

He nodded. They went out and walked by the Mississippi. This wasn't the big river that Mark Twain wrote about. Up here, north of the Missouri and Ohio, it was narrow and mostly clear. Big Muddy's mud came later, when the Missouri flowed in.

The water was blue from the sky and brown from tannin that leached out of North Woods peat bogs. It gave the river a deep, rich, reddish color. Big Brown Mama liked the hue, which reminded her of herself. She was that color sometimes. And she liked the sky blue, which reminded her of Big Blue Poppa, a special friend.

A couple of mallards floated close to the shore, and pigeons flew around a nearby bridge.

"I've seen lots of eagles here," the rabbit man said. "They give me the shakes. They'll eat rabbits if they get the chance, though they prefer fish or carrion."

Big Brown Mama stopped and put her hand on the rabbit man's chest. Nokomis was right, Everything was mixed up inside: man and rabbit, clay and railroad grease. She could feel the Georgia pine woods and the northern forest, the Detroit factories and Chicago clubs, even the neat houses of Rondo before the highway equipment came. She couldn't tell where one stopped and another began. This wasn't going to be easy.

Well, if she couldn't solve this problem in the present and she couldn't go into the past to solve it, that left one alternative. She grabbed the rabbit man by the arm and yanked him into the twenty-second century: not the end, when things began to get easier and there were hotels on the moon, but the middle of the century, when times could still be hard.

"Ow," he said as they arrived. "That hurt."

She let go of his arm, and he rubbed it, then looked around. "What the hell?"

They were still on the river bank, but the river was gone. A semi-tropical forest filled the river bed. Big Brown Mama could recognize the palms, but not the other trees. Maybe the low plants were cyclads. She was not a botanist.

"Where are we?" he asked, looking up the slope that rose from the river valley. Forest covered it. The only sign of humanity was a row of giant windmills on top of the river bluff, their blades turning in a hot, dry wind.

"St. Paul," said Big Brown Mama.

"Where's the Cathedral? And the State Capitol building? What happened to downtown? And what's wrong with the sun?"

It hung in the middle of a hazy sky, its light oddly dim.

"That's mostly dust," said Big Brown Mama. "When the wind comes form the south, as it's doing right now, it has to cross a lot of desert. But some of it's the parasol array. There's scientists who say that the dimming the array causes is so little no one can see it. But I can."

"The para-what?"

"They are structures in space. They look like parasols, except they are huge, and the things that look like handles are short. They orbit between the sun and Earth. We can't see them from here, but they cut the sunlight, and that makes the planet cooler. People now work mighty hard to undo the harm done in your time."

"Don't blame me," the rabbit man said. "I'll bet there weren't a lot of black folks — or rabbits — making the big decisions about global warming."

"Condoleezza Rice was on the board of directors of Chevron," Big Brown Mama replied. "And she had a tanker named after her."

"That's one person."

"Come on," said Big Brown Mama. "There's someone I want you to meet."

They walked uphill into the forest. Wood chip paths wandered under the trees, and there were buildings in the green shadows. Most were half-buried and looked hobbit-like, though the doors and windows were rectangular.

Gardens grew in clearings, where the dim sunlight poured in. People worked in the gardens. Other folks sped past on bicycles with fat, cross-country tires.

"This is damn strange," said the rabbit man.

"It's sustainable," Big Brown Mama replied.

They reached a building that wasn't buried in the ground, though it was low with log walls and a turf roof. A sign above the door said, "One-Day Genetic Analysis."

Big Brown Mama pushed open the door. They walked into a small store. Shelves lined the side walls. Scattered on them were models of complex molecules and extinct animals: dinosaurs, mammoths, armored fishes, and things that looked like scorpions, except they were flat and even creepier looking than scorpions.

A dinosaur with feathered arms and a long feathered tail stood next to a twisting object that was almost certainly DNA. Big Brown Mama could not identify the other molecules. She did better with the extinct animals. She had seen them when alive, and they looked a lot better in flesh and blood than they did as dusty little figurines.

A counter ran across the back of the store, and a woman stood behind it. She straightened up as they entered. If features were any indication, she was of African descent, though ancestry didn't matter a lot in this era. The woman's skin was bright blue, and a crest of shimmering, indigo feathers covered her head. The crest was down when Big Brown Mama came in. As soon as the blue person saw her, the feathers went up and bristled. "You!"

"Yes indeed. I want a quick and cheap genetic analysis."

"You?" the blue woman asked eagerly.

"No. You aren't going to get a look at my genome. This man here."

The woman looked at him dubiously. "He doesn't look interesting."

"Don't you believe it," Big Brown Mama said. "Just take a swab and see what you find."

The woman hesitated, then reached under her counter and came up with a swab. "Come over here and open up," she said to the rabbit man.

He did. She swabbed the inside of his cheek. "I can have the result by nine tonight."

"Good," said Big Brown Mama. "Maybe then I'll know what I'm up against."

"What does that mean?" the blue woman asked.

"None of your business."

They left and walked farther up the hill, coming finally to an open-air cafe. Metal chairs stood next to tables made from good-sized tree stumps. The sides were still bark-covered. There was even a little moss.

"This place gives me the creeps," the rabbit man said as they sat down.

"Why?"

"This is supposed to be a city."

"There are 100,000 people in St. Paul and Minneapolis, which is a lot for a city this far south. Most people live in Canada and Siberia or in the far south, Patagonia and Antarctica. Those are the green places with rain.

"The middle of the planet is desert, except for the western Sahara, which is wet and green. Something to do with the pattern of the winds."

A waitress arrived, a slim young woman over two meters tall. She wore green shorts and a yellow sleeveless shirt. Her skin was as green as the shorts; and her long, silky, floating hair was the same bright yellow as her shirt.

In Big Brown Mama's opinion, she looked like an ear of corn. This was not bad. Big Brown Mama liked corn, especially new and boiled, with salt and a lot of butter. The rabbit man looked at the waitress briefly, then glanced away, clearly uncomfortable. Maybe he wasn't a fan of corn.

They ordered. The waitress left.

"Fortunately, there was a population drop," Big Brown Mama said after the waitress left. "The planet can still support humanity, even with all the areas that have dried up or been drowned. The oceans are five meters higher than in your day. A lot of low lands and islands have gone underwater."

"How much?" the rabbit man asked.

"Did the population drop? It's 900 million now. The twenty-first century was *hard*."

"I'll bet a lot more poor people died than rich people, and a lot more brown people than white people."

"Yes," said Big Brown Mama. "Fortunately humans are almost identical genetically, so very little information was lost."

"Except the information in the minds of the people who died," said the rabbit man. "You are a cold, hard woman."

"I am a woman who has seen more than you can imagine."

The waitress returned with coffee and sandwiches. The rabbit man wolfed down his veggie delight, then drank coffee while Big Brown Mama investigated the dessert tray. She picked something that was dense chocolate topped with cream.

"Goat cream," she told the rabbit man. "Cows are not energy efficient, and they fart too much methane. So they are gone, except a small number in historical zoos."

The rabbit man shuddered. "How did this happen?"

"The usual way. Greed and stupidity. But humanity survived." Big Brown Mama polished off her dense chocolate and licked cream off her spoon. "You have a lot of political opinions for an archetype. Most archetypes don't go in for political analysis, at least in my experience."

"I've been a man a long time, and I studied with the Communists in the 1930s."

They walked around, looking at the city under the trees, then went down to the Mississippi. A small river—barely more than a stream—ran through the middle of its bed.

"I could wade this," said the rabbit man. "The mighty Mississippi. Hunh!"

The dim sun kept moving west, and the river valley filled with shadow. At nine they went back to the gene shop. The blue woman was there, looking upset.

"What is he?" she asked Big Brown Mama, while pointing at the rabbit man.

"What do you mean?"

"He's got rabbit genes in his DNA, and I don't mean just a few. This man is seriously lagomorphic."

"You should talk," the rabbit man said. "You have feathers."

"That is purely cosmetic. But you are a chimera."

"Wait a minute," he said. "You just called me lago-something."

"You are a lagomorphic chimera, a mixture of human and rabbit genes; and that is illegal. It's one thing to add a few genes for decoration, but deep-down changes, real genetic mixing—no! We don't allow that kind of thing on Earth."

The rabbit man shrugged, looking angry.

"And that's not all." The blue woman glared at Big Brown Mama. "Rabbit genes may be illegal, but there's nothing hard about adding them to human DNA. In fact it's easy, which is why we have gene police. If we didn't, every fool would be making chimeras.

"But he has *petroleum* in his DNA. Genetically speaking, he is partly a man, partly a rabbit, and partly a thick, viscous, flammable mixture of hydrocarbons. This is flat out impossible, and I don't like it one bit. In addition—" Her voice rose.

"There is more?" asked Big Brown Mama pleasantly.

"There is *silicon dioxide* in his genome. This man's DNA is sandy."

"As well as oily," Big Brown Mama said in an interested tone.

The blue woman nodded.

"That seems pretty harmless," Big Brown Mama said. "If there's sand, ain't no one gonna slip on the oil."

"It's not natural, nor is it legal. I want no part of it."

"Does that mean you don't want to be paid?"

The blue woman hesitated. "I would like my fee."

Big Brown Mama always came prepared. She handed over a credit disk, and the woman processed the sale. "I'm going to have to report him to the gene police. Maybe I am wrong about the petroleum and silica. My analysis *was* quick and dirty. There might be contamination. I'm willing to admit that much. But I am right about the rabbit. This man is *mixed*."

"I'll say," said Big Brown Mama. "Part rabbit, part man, part grease, and part clay, and it's showing at the genetic level. I did not expect that. Thank you for your help."

"I'm calling the cops right now," the blue woman said.

Big Brown Mama opened the shop door. "Do what you need to, sweetie."

They walked out into early evening. A full moon, huge and dim orange, hung in the dark blue sky. Lightning bugs flashed around them.

"There's a lot more of those bugs than I remember being in St. Paul," said the rabbit man.

"They've been moving north, along with a lot of other animals and plants."

"What now?"

"I've been wondering what would happen if I yanked you out. It seemed likely you'd leave something behind—the man part, and you told me you wanted to keep that."

"I want to keep the memories."

"You can't separate a man from his memories or memories from the man. But now it seems as if everything you are has dug itself into your DNA. I don't think you're going to lose it."

A pair of flashing blue lights came up the hill toward them, moving quickly. When they were a little closer, Big Brown Mama made out two men on bicycles. They were peddling fiercely. The flashing blue lights were fastened on their helmets.

"The gene police," she said. "Let's go."

She took the rabbit man's hand and pulled him back to the start of the twenty-first century. It was night here as well, but light shone from the downtown skyscrapers and from the excursion boats docked at Harriet Island across the river. The river was full-sized again. Its dark surface glimmered with reflections.

Big Brown Mama turned in a circle. The St. Paul Cathedral was back, its high dome spotlit, and—off to the right—the white State Capitol building shone like a statue carved from fresh butter.

"I like this better," the rabbit man said.

"Like it while you can," Big Brown Mama said. "Its time is almost done."

She looked at her companion closely. Her night vision was good; and she had no trouble seeing the man or his ghostly rabbit ears, which glowed faintly. "Do you know any light bulb jokes?" she asked.

"Not that I can remember."

"This one is my favorite. 'How many therapists does it take to change a light bulb?'"

The rabbit man looked irritated. "What kind of question is that?"

"'One, but the light bulb has to really want to change.' There's a point to that joke. You are an archetype, and that means you have power. Ma Johnson got you confused, and maybe your own wants and needs got you confused. You wanted to go north; and you wanted to be a man; and then you got trapped in what you wanted. A person—even an archetype—can get stuck in his own thinking like an animal in the famous La Brea tar pits in California.

"But you still have power, and you need to use it now. When I pull, you are going to have to will yourself free, along with every part you want to keep. If you don't help, I'm not sure what will come out. Maybe just the original Brer Rabbit. Given your DNA, I think I'm going to get a mixture. But will it be the right mixture? Who do you want to be?"

"I want my memories," the rabbit man said stubbornly.

"Well, then. Will hard." She reached out and grasped the rabbit ears. The man winced, then scrunched up his face, willing fiercely.

"Here goes," said Big Brown Mama, and she pulled as hard as she could.

Something made a snapping noise. For a moment, the man stood perfectly still, his face frozen in a scrunched expression. Then his body split in two from crown to crotch. The two parts fell to either side, hit the sidewalk pavement, and shattered. Big Brown Mama was standing in front of a heap of broken pieces of unfired clay.

"Well, now," she exclaimed. In her hand was a pair of rabbit ears, no longer ghostly, and attached to the ears was a large, rangy rabbit that kicked its long legs, trying to get free.

She bent and set the rabbit down. It took several hops away from her, then stopped and sat upright. Its nose twitched. Its long ears flicked. It looked at her with dark, intelligent eyes.

"Who are you?" Big Brown Mama asked.

The rabbit swelled up and out, rising till it was six feet tall and broad through the shoulders. For a moment, it looked like something between a rabbit and a man: man-sized and man-shaped, but covered with fur and with long, rabbit ears. Then it flickered and was entirely a man. He even had clothes on: jeans and a tee-shirt and big, black, shiny, lace-up work boots. The boots were new and an improvement. He was remembering his power, Big Brown Mama thought with approval, and he was remembering how important good work boots are. A man — or rabbit — could wreck his feet in bad shoes.

"Nanabozho can do this," the rabbit man said. "And now so can I."

"Well," said Big Brown Mama again, then asked, "How much did you keep?"

"Georgia," the rabbit man said after a brief reflection. "The pine woods and cotton fields and people sitting and talking on their porches in the evening. I never realized how hard life was for them. I was just a rabbit then. But I liked their music and the vegetables in their gardens. I don't know if I'd be able to eat those gardens now. I've been a man too long. Stealing from poor folks seems wrong.

"I remember Detroit. I don't think there's any way to forget the Rouge Plant. It's sitting in my mind as solid as it was in reality. You know—they tore it down, like most of the plants in Detroit. But it's still in here." He tapped his head.

"Ma Johnson and her magic. Chicago and Rondo. It's all in here." He tapped his head a second time. The rabbit ears were gone, Big Brown Mama noticed. No. There they were again, flicking back and forth.

"What are you going to do?" she asked.

"Go up north and find Nanabozho. He will appreciate this." He spread his arms wide, indicating his transformation. "Go fishing. Run in the woods. I'll have to be careful. There are wolves up north. If I'm lucky, I'll find the kind of cabin that rich folks build and take a look at the garden. It isn't wrong to steal from the rich. That's redistribution.

"And then—" He paused, looking at the river. "I think I'll come back down here. There's a part of me that likes fixing machinery and listening to jazz. No reason to give that up, just because I'm Brer Rabbit again. Maybe I can find myself a woman. Brer Rabbit likes making trouble more than sex. But the man part of me is exactly the opposite." He grinned. "I'd forgotten that. I've been feeling pretty low in recent years. Too low to love. But now—"

"That sounds like too ordinary a life for an archetype," Big Brown Mama said. She was drawing on her own experience. She liked a lot of excitement.

"Nothing wrong with ordinary, if it's what you chose. Maybe I'll join a neighborhood organization or go work for the Obama campaign. The rabbit part of me has no interest in politics, but the man part would like to see a black president."

"You will," said Big Brown Mama. "But you'll find he's not a solution to what ails this planet."

"Then maybe I will listen to my inner rabbit and cause some trouble. I don't know if we're stuck with the future you showed me. It's better than complete ruin, but I hate the thought of so many people dying; and it seems to me folks could create a bigger future, something with more scope."

He looked serious for a moment, then his grin came back. "You wouldn't think it was such a big deal, to be free of that oil and red Georgia clay. But I feel as if everything is opening up for me. You are right about my power. I have it, and now I believe I can use it. Thank you for what you've done." He shrank down into a rabbit and hopped away.

Big Brown Mama watched him go with her excellent night vision. Hard to tell what she had created or freed. Time would tell.

Thinking of time, she decided to go back to the future, and the hotel on the moon at the end of twenty-second century.

She did exactly that, sending a message to Big Blue Poppa en route. They met on the moon and had a fine old time. He stood out a little, since most people had gone back to looking the way people used to. But there were enough eccentrics so a sky-blue man with long, curly, indigo hair was striking but not shocking. After a week, they parted with a kiss, and both went off to other places and times.

One day, 150 years later, she was sitting in a jazz bar in Barsoom City on Mars. Outside, beyond the dome that covered BC, it was summer in the southern hemisphere. The temp was a mild zero Centigrade. The day was clear, except for a handful of high, thin clouds and the usual haze of dust. None of this was evident where she sat, but she had checked the weather on her phone and taken a long look at the bare, red plain beyond the city: tiny on the phone's screen, but satisfyingly alien. There was no point in being on another planet if you didn't pay attention.

A pair of Martian natives were up on a stage, fiddling with sound equipment and some odd-looking instruments. Like most humans native to Mars, they were over two meters tall, thin as rails, and black as coal. The skin color was protection against radiation on a planet with too little atmosphere. The rest was fashion. All the science fiction stories said Martians were tall and thin; and so they were, thanks to gene mod. Looking alike helped create a sense of solidarity.

Like most Martians, they wore coveralls dotted with badges: the places they had been, the clubs and teams they belonged to. Martians were into affiliation and achievement, so long as the achievement was not boasting. They didn't like to boast or put down other people, especially other Martians.

She sipped her Chardonnay and thought about life on Mars: the human colonists and their animals and plants, the native microbes that lived far underground in cracks in the rock. Interestingly, the two kinds of life were related. One planet had colonized the other early in the solar system's history. Most likely, Mars was the planet of origin; and now her children had come home to a world where there was no surface life and the most complex organisms were slimes and bubbles living in volcanic vents.

At that point, as she was considering the history of life in the solar system, a tall, black man with rabbit ears came in. He looked younger and handsomer than he had when she last saw him, but those ears were distinctive.

"Looking good," she said as he passed her table.

He stopped. "Do I know you?"

"You used to."

He took a closer look. "The lady who travels through time!"

She nodded.

He grinned. "Can I sit down?"

She nodded again. He sat. A robot waiter glided over and took his order. After the robot was gone, she said, "You learned more about your power."

"Well, I never learned how to travel in time, except the way most people do—going toward the future at a speed of one second per second. But I got here finally. You were right about Obama and the twenty-first century. A pair of ugly messes. I'm glad both are over. The twenty-second century was better, and this one seems to be turning out well. Though Nanabozho is still heartbroken about losing so much of his northern forest." He paused, reflecting. "Anansi and Monkey aren't happy about what happened to their parts of the world. Only person who is satisfied is Coyote. He can live in a desert. Hell, he can live anywhere, and I hate to say it, he has a mean streak. Humanity's suffering does not bother him."

The robot brought beer and a sandwich. The rabbit man tucked in.

"Why are you here?" asked Big Brown Mama.

"I came for the big Martian trade union conference."

"Are you a Martian now?" asked Big Brown Mama with surprise. He didn't look Martian, in spite of being black. He was too broad and solid, the way Big Brown Mama liked a man. Humans ought to have meat on their bones.

"Nope. I represent a rank-and-file insurgent movement on Earth that intends to kick the ass of the Earth Central Labor Council if those fools don't start behaving as if they have some guts and common sense. We are looking for allies on other worlds."

"It's a long way to come."

"That's the trouble with worlds. They aren't put close together, except Earth and the Moon. But people are spreading out from Earth to Mars and beyond. I figure I ought to take myself—and the things I believe in—at least part of the way. You can never tell when humanity is going to need an archetype.

"After I finish here, I'm heading for Jupiter. They're building a star ship there. The labor is union. I want to meet some of them and some of the ship's crew, who are also union. There's a part of me that would like to go, but it's a long trip and likely to be boring.

"I'll take a later ship, after they get the speed up."

Big Brown Mama shook her head. "I never saw you as a starman *or* a union organizer."

He wolfed down the rest of his sandwich. When he was done chewing and swallowing, he asked, "How much time have you spent in the twenty-first century?"

"Not a lot," said Big Brown Mama, feeling a little defensive. Why should she spend time in the twenty-first century when she had the option of skipping it? She liked progress and good times.

The rabbit man nodded, as if he'd been expecting her answer. "Everything started to collapse right around the time you set me free, and it kept collapsing, like an avalanche going down a mountain—slowing down sometimes, hanging up on a level place and seeming to be over, then beginning to slide again. Down and down, while all the ice on the planet melted, and the oceans rose.

"A lot of old ideas came back then. *Solidarity forever. All power to the people. Bread, peace, and land. The working class and the employing class have nothing in common.* —Funny, how that was. All at once, those worn-out, used-up slogans made sense again, when people were living in Obamavilles or dying of hunger in countries where it no longer rained.

"It wasn't just the ruined economy that brought the ideas back, or the damaged planet. It was how hard the people on top were willing to fight to keep what they had, even if it meant that most of the planet was going to die.

"It was pretty clear what they were planning—a ruined planet with them in their enclaves and L-5 colonies, being cared for by machinery and human servants, while the rest of us lived in misery, if we stayed alive at all.

"It was a terrible vision of the future. My inner rabbit told me to jump in and do something. My human self told me I ought to cause *human* trouble. Duking it out with Brer Fox and Brer Bear or trying to out-trick Brer Spider did not seem enough for Modern Times.

"So I became an organizer, like the Reds I knew in Detroit in the twentieth century. I didn't stay at one job, partly because I got bored and partly because people would notice that I don't get old, if I stayed long enough. But there's always some new project, some new fight. When I get tired, I take a break in what forest is left, or I get a job as a handy person. I can still fix almost any kind of machine.

"But mostly I make trouble, the way I always have."

"Do you still see Nanabozho?" She had liked the sound of the tall Indian with rabbit ears.

"Uh-huh. He's more of an environmentalist than I am, working to save his forests. Me, I figure you can't save the planet unless you save the people on it. So I concentrate on them.

"But we both—we all—fight. There's not going to be any place for archetypes unless we can save what we represent." He leaned back, his hands around his glass of beer. They were big and strong and worn-looking. Big Brown Mama noted this with approval. She liked hands that showed hard work; and she liked people who didn't forget what they had been.

"*La lucha continua,*" the rabbit man said finally. "This beer is pretty good. Let's listen to some jazz."

Afterword

I don't know if American kids still learn tall tales. I did: Paul Bunyan and Babe the Blue Ox, John Henry, Mike Fink the keelboat pilot, Joe Magarac the steel worker. They were working people, most of them men. (Though I just learned about Annie Christmas, a keelboat pilot who could toss Mike Fink around. According to one source I found, Annie was six feet seven inches tall and weighed 250 pounds. Her moustache was blond and curly and was the finest, widest moustache on the Mississippi. Another source told me that Annie was African American.) The tall tale heroes were bigger, taller, tougher, and stronger than anyone else. They built America, cutting timber, laying track, moving cargo on the big American rivers, and pouring steel.

Remember that I grew up in the shadow of the Great Depression and World War II and at a time when American unions were strong. The idea of building America was important, and it was easy to see the people who built the country with their own hands as heroic. I associate tall tale heroes with WPA art and posters like Rosie the Riveter saying, "We Can Do It." I don't know who our heroes are today.

A number of years ago I began to wonder what space-age tall tales would be like. I wanted something as over the top as a classic Paul Bunyan story, but set in a science fictional environment. This led to "Big Black Mama and Tentacle Man." I enjoyed writing it, so I wrote more Big Mama stories. Like Paul Bunyan and the rest, the Big Mamas are bigger, taller, tougher, and stronger than anyone else. They come in all the colors that humans do, as well as many additional colors. Unlike most of the heroes I learned about as a kid, they are women, though — as I keep pointing out — there are Big Poppas. They even show up now and then.

The Mamas are closer to tricksters than they are to the usual tall tale heroes, using a certain amount of intelligence to solve their problems. I suppose I could have created a character like Annie Christmas, who solves her problems with sheer muscle and grit, but I haven't yet.

The last Big Mama story, "Big Brown Mama and Brer Rabbit," is my answer to all the fantasies that put European folklore into America: Irish fairy courts in Minneapolis or New York, for example. I asked myself, "Why can't people write about the magical creatures native to the US?" I decided to write about Brer Rabbit, because he's hard to beat as a trickster, though — like all tricksters — he is sometimes outwitted or outwits himself

So here is my contribution to American folklore in the early years of the space age. Don't tell me I have to be a folk to make this kind of contribution. I am as much of a folk as you are.

And don't worry about my ideas about time travel. That part of every story is BS.

Author Biography

Eleanor Arnason was born in New York City in 1942. Her mother, Elizabeth Hickcox Yard, was a social worker who grew up in a missionary community in western China. Her father, Hjorvardur Harvard Arnason, was the son of Icelandic immigrants and an art historian. She grew up in New York, Chicago, London, Paris, Washington DC, Honolulu, St. Paul, and Minneapolis. She received a BA in art history from Swarthmore College and did graduate work at the University of Minnesota, before quitting to learn about life outside art museums and institutions of higher learning. She made her first professional sale in 1972 while living in the Detroit inner city. Since then she has published five novels and over thirty works of short fiction. Her fourth novel, *A Woman of the Iron People* (2001), won the James Tiptree, Jr. award for gender-bending science fiction and the Mythopoeic Society Award for adult fantasy. Her fifth novel, *Ring of Swords* (1995), won a Minnesota Book Award. Since 1994 she has devoted herself to short fiction. Her story "Dapple" won the Spectrum Award for GLBT science fiction and was a finalist for the Sturgeon Award. Other stories have been finalists for the World Fantasy, Hugo, and Nebula Awards, and for the Sturgeon and Sidewise Awards.

She lives in Minnesota and is currently a full time writer. Her interests include politics, economics, bird-watching, and hanging out in local coffee shops.